The Heirs
Three foster sis...
inherited

There was a dangerous edge to Cade McKnight, one that Delia didn't understand.

For all his casual smiles and laughter, there remained a part of him that was always prepared for anything. Maybe it was the bright day, or the isolation, but she thought she saw a surprising depth to him now, and it made her take a good, long look at him.

He looked back just as steadily, without a hint of discomfort.

Hurt, she realized, startled. He was hiding a wealth of hurt just beneath his rough surface, and this unexpected side to the man she'd thought of only as a pain in her own rear end was unsettling.

She looked away first.

Dear Reader,

As you have no doubt noticed, this year marks Silhouette Books' 20th anniversary, and for the next three months the spotlight shines on Intimate Moments, so we've packed our schedule with irresistible temptations.

First off, I'm proud to announce that this month marks the beginning of A YEAR OF LOVING DANGEROUSLY, a twelve-book continuity series written by eleven of your favorite authors. Sharon Sala, a bestselling, award-winning, absolutely incredible writer, launches things with *Mission: Irresistible,* and next year she will also write the final book in the continuity. Picture a top secret agency, headed by a man no one sees. Now picture a traitor infiltrating security, chased by a dozen (or more!) of the agency's best operatives. The trail crisscrosses the globe, and passion is a big part of the picture, until the final scene is played out and the final romance reaches its happy conclusion. Every book in A YEAR OF LOVING DANGEROUSLY features a self-contained romance, along with a piece of the ongoing puzzle, and enough excitement and suspense to fuel your imagination for the entire year. Don't miss a single monthly installment!

This month also features new books from top authors such as Beverly Barton, who continues THE PROTECTORS, and Marie Ferrarella, who revisits THE BABY OF THE MONTH CLUB. And in future months look for *New York Times* bestselling author Linda Howard, with *A Game of Chance* (yes, it's Chance Mackenzie's story at long last), and a special in-line two-in-one collection by Maggie Shayne and Marilyn Pappano, called *Who Do You Love?* All that and more of A YEAR OF LOVING DANGEROUSLY, as well as new books from the authors who've made Intimate Moments *the* place to come for a mix of excitement and romance no reader can resist. Enjoy!

Leslie J. Wainger
Executive Senior Editor

Please address questions and book requests to:
Silhouette Reader Service
U.S.: 3010 Walden Ave., P.O. Box 1325, Buffalo, NY 14269
Canadian: P.O. Box 609, Fort Erie, Ont. L2A 5X3

THE DETECTIVE'S UNDOING

JILL SHALVIS

Silhouette®

INTIMATE™ MOMENTS®

Published by Silhouette Books

America's Publisher of Contemporary Romance

To Megan, warrior princess

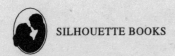 SILHOUETTE BOOKS

ISBN 0-373-27089-5

THE DETECTIVE'S UNDOING

Copyright © 2000 by Jill Shalvis

This edition published by arrangement with Harlequin Books S.A.

® and TM are trademarks of Harlequin Books S.A., used under license.
Trademarks indicated with ® are registered in the United States Patent
and Trademark Office, the Canadian Trade Marks Office and in other
countries.

Visit Silhouette at www.eHarlequin.com

Printed in U.S.A.

JILL SHALVIS

When pressed for an answer on why she writes romance, Jill Shalvis just smiles and says she didn't realize there was anything else. She's written over a dozen novels so far and doesn't plan on stopping. She lives in California, in a house filled with young children, too many animals and her hero/husband. Jill loves to hear from readers, and can be reached at P.O. Box 3945, Truckee, CA 96160.

IT'S OUR 20th ANNIVERSARY!
We'll be celebrating all year,
Continuing with these fabulous titles,
On sale in July 2000.

Intimate Moments

 #1015 Egan Cassidy's Kid
Beverly Barton

 #1016 Mission: Irresistible
Sharon Sala

 #1017 The Once and Future Father
Marie Ferrarella

#1018 Imminent Danger
Carla Cassidy

 #1019 The Detective's Undoing
Jill Shalvis

#1020 Who's Been Sleeping in Her Bed?
Pamela Dalton

Special Edition

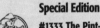 **#1333 The Pint-Sized Secret**
Sherryl Woods

#1334 Man of Passion
Lindsay McKenna

#1335 Whose Baby Is This?
Patricia Thayer

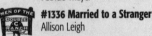 **#1336 Married to a Stranger**
Allison Leigh

#1337 Doctor and the Debutante
Pat Warren

#1338 Maternal Instincts
Beth Henderson

Desire

 #1303 Bachelor Doctor
Barbara Boswell

 #1304 Midnight Fantasy
Ann Major

#1305 Wife for Hire
Amy J. Fetzer

 #1306 Ride a Wild Heart
Peggy Moreland

#1307 Blood Brothers
Anne McAllister & Lucy Gordon

#1308 Cowboy for Keeps
Kristi Gold

Romance

#1456 Falling for Grace
Stella Bagwell

 #1457 The Borrowed Groom
Judy Christenberry

#1458 Denim & Diamond
Moyra Tarling

 #1459 The Monarch's Son
Valerie Parv

 #1460 Jodie's Mail-Order Man
Julianna Morris

#1461 Lassoed!
Martha Shields

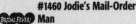

Prologue

At six years old, Delia Scanlon knew everything she needed to about control.

Having it was the only way to survive.

As she hung upside down from a low branch on the tree outside the group home where she lived, her long blond hair swept the grass. Next to her hung her two foster sisters, Zoe and Maddie.

Actually, Maddie wasn't hanging; the quiet, sweet little girl was too timid for that. She sat, gripping the branch for all she was worth, very carefully watching the ground beneath her.

Zoe, who was not quiet or sweet, hung by one leg, calmly inspecting the torn knees of her jeans. Upside down, she popped a huge bubble and casually said, "I've got three lollipops under my pillow."

Delia's mouth watered and she went all warm and fuzzy inside. She knew Zoe would share—that's how it was between them. Maddie and Zoe were more than her foster sisters; they were her *life*.

It wasn't easy being in the group home with too many kids and too few caretakers, but they were fed and clothed and safe. And they had each other. It was enough for Delia, who just wanted to be with Zoe and Maddie. They were family, no matter what everyone told them.

"When I marry a prince," she announced, "he'll take us away on his white horse. We'll live in a beautiful castle where we can eat all the macaroni and cheese we want."

"Will you have horses?" Zoe asked, snapping her gum.

"Lots. You'll come?"

Zoe smiled dreamily. "Yeah."

"Maddie?"

"I go anywhere you go."

Delia, with her natural maternal instinct, liked the thought of taking care of her sisters for the rest of her life. "The three of us together."

Maddie nodded solemnly.

Zoe flipped down from the tree and tossed back her hair. "I get to be in charge of the horses."

"Sure." Delia thought horses were dirty and smelled funny, but she wanted Zoe with her, so she'd promise her anything. "What do you want, Maddie?"

"To be a family," Maddie said softly, her eyes shining with the dream.

"Always," Delia vowed, as if she had the power to make it so. "Always."

Content with that, they sat on the grass in the hot Los Angeles sun, holding hands and thinking about their happily-ever-after.

A thousand miles away on a rugged isolated Idaho ranch, Constance Freeman was searching for her stolen granddaughter. Well not *stolen* exactly—the law didn't consider it stealing when the baby's own father, who had custody rights, had done the taking. But Constance didn't fool herself; her son had no business with a baby, and her heart ached just thinking about what that poor child might have gone through in the past six long years.

Her vengeful son hadn't so much as written, and Constance yearned to know the fate of her own flesh and blood.

She stared down at a map of the United States, her brow furrowed as she wondered for the thousandth time where they'd gone.

There was the Triple M ranch, her pride and joy, to run but, in Constance's mind it had taken a backseat to finding her granddaughter. *Everything* would take a backseat, until she had the child where she belonged.

On Triple Mountain.

Chapter 1

Twenty years later

He was stuck.

Stuck, while the powerful wanderlust within him tore him apart, driving him crazy with the need to roam far and free.

It wasn't a physical sort of stuck. He couldn't imagine anything as simple as that keeping him in one place.

No, it was a promise that held him, his own promises, no less.

The woman he'd made the promise to, Constance Freeman, was dead. But to Cade McKnight, a vow of any kind was as good as gold. He'd never broken one before, and he didn't intend to start now.

But with all his heart and soul he wanted to be free of the promise.

It was past midnight, but he'd been unable to sleep. A long hard ride in the saddle hadn't helped.

It took only a second to let himself in the huge ranch-style house that would serve as the main lodge when there were guests at the Triple M. There were no guests yet, but four people—three of them his friends and one a complete baffling mystery—owned and operated the place, and lived here.

They were sleeping now. Grateful for the silence and the time to think and yearn, Cade stood just inside the front door.

A sound drifted from the sleeping house, from the kitchen. Not a normal sound, but a choked nearly silent whisper.

Tense, Cade moved lithely through the large living room, coming to a stop just outside the double swinging doors to the kitchen.

No light was on.

The Triple M Guest Ranch was a fairly secure place, located in the vast wilds of western Idaho hundreds of miles from the nearest big city. But Cade, who was not a country boy but rather a certified city rat, never took chances.

Especially when he had friends sleeping upstairs. He cared about those three friends, Zoe, Maddie and Ty—and that one baffling mystery, too—far more than he wanted to.

Which reminded him of how much he wished

he was clutching a one-way ticket out of here. He was chomping at the bit to get moving once more.

The sound came again.

Cade shoved his way through the double wooden doors and turned on the overhead light all in one movement.

Blinking in the sudden light was that one mystery—the cool calm Delia Scanlon.

She was stunningly, shockingly beautiful. Alabaster skin. Long thick luxurious pale blond hair that fell in waves past her shoulders. Full sensuous lips guaranteed to drive a man wild.

She stood in front of the opened refrigerator, bathed in the white light of the refrigerator bulb, her lush curves not entirely concealed by her surprisingly plain terry-cloth bathrobe.

Her eyes, the color of a brilliant mountain sky, seared through him.

They were tear-ravaged.

He swore, hating the way his heart twisted from just looking at her. He hated having his heart do anything, but to have it *feel,* and feel so passionately, suitably terrified him so that he stood rock still and offered no comfort. "What are you doing?"

"Me? Oh, just dancing with the moon." Turning away, she wiped at the tears he had pretended not to see and she had pretended not to have shed.

The hunch of her usually ramrod-straight shoulders tore at him and, furious with himself, he turned his back on her. "Dammit, next time flip the light on or something. I thought you were—"

"What? A burglar out in the middle of nowhere? Get a grip, McKnight." Her voice, with its low grainy sexy tone of a 1930s movie siren, sounded full of temper.

That was good, he told himself. Temper was far preferable to tears.

"Go away," she said.

She still hadn't looked at him, but then again, he wasn't looking at her, either. He couldn't.

If he did, he'd feel that strange inexplicable absolutely unacceptable tug. He didn't want to believe it was attraction, didn't want to believe it was anything, so he ignored it.

So did she.

It suited them both. Delia was no more country than he was, raised as she'd been in the Los Angeles child-welfare system. He knew this, not because they talked much—by tacit agreement they avoided each other—but because he was the private investigator who'd promised Constance Freeman he'd find her long-lost granddaughter, heir to the Triple M.

It should have been an easy open-and-shut case. But of course, given his luck of the past few years, it hadn't been. He'd found an heir all right, *three* of them. Delia, Maddie and Zoe, all foster sisters, dumped into the system at approximately the same time and age.

It was his job to narrow the choices down to the correct woman, a feat that had so far escaped him.

"Stop staring at me," Delia said.

He glanced over his shoulder to find her still glaring into the refrigerator. "I'm not even looking at you."

"You are so."

He smiled then, because they were both obviously tired, cranky and...well, he didn't want to think about what else they were. Because whatever it was, they were it together and he didn't want anything to do with it.

"Why don't you just leave?" She was again looking into the refrigerator, scowling hard, as if she could find the answers to world peace and hunger, but it was her voice that reached him. She sounded confused and hurt, and he had an insane urge to soothe her.

"You know I can't," he said, wishing yet again that he could.

She pushed at a jar of mayonnaise and peered behind it, searching. "You've proven Zoe isn't the heir."

"Which still leaves you and Maddie."

She pulled out an apple and examined it, then rejected it. "Not me. You know it's not me."

"I know no such thing."

"My father was a cop." Her fingers turned white with their death grip on a bottle of soda. "An undercover cop who never knew of my existence, remember? You yourself found this out just last week when you tracked down my so-called birth mother and found out that she was dead.''

Because he sensed the fragile hold she had on her emotions, he stayed where he was and said quietly, ''Yes, I remember.'' He also remembered how she'd looked when he'd told her, the shattered emotions that had swum in her expressive eyes when she'd realized her mother was gone forever, the mother who'd left her in a foster home.

She didn't look shattered now, but with the tears wiped away, she looked strong. Fiercely independent. And despite himself, admiration filled him for her ability to roll with the punches life had thrown her.

He, more than anyone, knew exactly how painful those punches could be.

''And Constance's no-good jerk of a son was a drifter,'' she continued. ''Not a cop. So really, I couldn't be her granddaughter.''

''I don't think your mother was real good at truths, Delia,'' he said gently.

That had her snapping her gaze back to his, but when she spoke, it was not with the heat of temper, but with the slow precision that only pain and sorrow could bring. ''I'd like to be able to deny that.''

It was a surprising admission from a woman who'd been very careful to keep herself hidden from him. He understood perfectly, as the attempt was mutual. ''I'm on the case until I have answers.''

She muttered something, but he missed it. When

he raised a brow in question, she sighed with ex-
asperation.

"I said thank you for finding my half brother."

Given how she'd ground out each word, especially the "thank you" part, Cade knew how difficult the words had been. For some reason, this
lightened his mood, made him want to grin. "I'm
sorry...what was that?" He ignored her growl of
frustration and cupped a hand to his ear, giving her
an innocent smile.

"Thank you," she said again through her teeth.
Then she swallowed, hard, and all traces of resentment vanished. Her voice and expression softened. "I didn't even know Jacob existed and I owe
you for that. I'm going next week to Los Angeles
to meet him for the first time and..."

"And...?"

"And I'm grateful, okay?"

She looked close to tears again, which he
couldn't take. Cocking his head, he ran his gaze
over the body that could make a grown man beg
and gave a wicked smile designed to claw at her
temper. "How grateful?" he asked.

For a second she gaped at him before her composure returned. It was fascinating to watch.

She was fascinating to watch.

Without a word, she sauntered past him, chin
high, walking regally from the kitchen into the re-
cesses of the dark house.

Which left him alone.

That was nothing new. He was always alone.

* * *

Learning to ride. Oh, the joy of it. *Not.*

The day stretched out before Delia, glorious and cloud-free. Good thing, too, because though it was only October, they'd been battered by a series of storms, and she was already a little tired of the bone-numbing cold.

She was also tired of worrying.

There was so much, she didn't know where to start. She worried about Maddie and Zoe and how hard they had to work. She worried about her newly found little brother, living far away in Los Angeles with a distant aunt, because no one had known to contact her. She worried about this big bad wilderness she was living in, when all she knew were shopping malls and Thai takeout. She worried about—

"Hey."

Him. She worried about him.

Silently cursing her sisters' good humor—which had included this so-called riding lesson, courtesy of one Cade McKnight—she shifted in her saddle and looked into Cade's mischievous eyes. As always, her heart skipped a beat, which annoyed her since her heart never skipped a beat over something as simple as a male.

"You're not paying attention," he said. "You're letting that horse have her way."

"I am not." But good old Betsy betrayed her, bending her long neck down to graze. Delia turned away from Cade's laughing gaze, trying to no avail to pull on Betsy's reins.

The horse continued to graze peacefully.

"Try harder. With authority."

Delia did...and broke a nail. She gritted her teeth and pulled harder.

Chewing complacently, Betsy twisted her neck and gazed balefully at Delia, but when she finished her mouthful, she didn't go for more. Instead, she shifted, as if considering taking off for a nice long run.

Delia's eyes widened slightly, her only concession to alarm. "Stop," she demanded of the suddenly restless Betsy, the gentlest horse on the Triple M.

Cade reached over and stroked Betsy's nose. "Shh, baby, it's okay."

"I know *I'm* okay." Delia said. "Talk to the horse!"

"I was." Cade grinned when Delia made a sound of frustration. "But you're looking pretty okay, too. *Baby.*"

She rolled her eyes and looked away. Anywhere but at Cade.

They were still on Triple M property, but far enough from the house and barns that the vast land before her felt like another world. The hills were dotted with early frost, and the Salmon River raged more loudly than her thoughts. There wasn't a freeway, let alone a car, in sight. No smog, no sirens, nothing. And to make it worse, she was sitting on a horse. A *horse,* for God's sake.

She missed her city.

Cade's lips curved as he tipped his head, studying her. A lock of wavy dark hair fell into his eyes, eyes that always seemed to see right through her icy calm to the Delia she didn't want exposed.

"You're thinking of your message," he said.

"Humph."

"The judge finally reviewed your request for custody of Jacob. You have a hearing set for next month."

Her greatest hope and terror all mixed into one. Oh, she definitely wanted Jacob, but what made her think Jacob wanted her?

Cade was watching her closely now, and she returned his stare with one of her own. He was tall and built like an athlete, with powerful muscles born more from physical labor than any gym. With the sun behind him, every one of those muscles was outlined beneath his dark T-shirt, along with the ones in his long legs, which were encompassed in faded snug denim. And every one of those muscles was tense as he sat in the saddle looking at her. "This is good news, remember?"

"Of course."

He bent closer, peering into her face. "Then where's the smile?"

Baring her teeth, she gave the smile her best shot.

His big body shifted back, but he still watched her with that probing gaze.

As if he knew.

She assured herself that her secret fear was safe.

No one must know that she was afraid and ashamed that she might be found lacking, not good enough to gain custody of her half brother.

But as she looked into Cade's melting brown eyes, eyes that were filled with questions, she swallowed hard.

She could trust him.

The thought came from nowhere and was quickly squelched.

With one click of his tongue, Cade moved his horse right next to hers. "Why were you crying last night?" he asked bluntly.

She closed her eyes, blocking out the pretty but too-cool autumn sun, the breeze and his too-curious gaze.

"Was it Jacob?"

She didn't—couldn't—answer.

"You don't have to go meet him alone," Cade said as if she'd responded. "Your sisters—"

"It's too expensive." And none of them had a spare cent to their name. "And then there's the upcoming opening. Plus, we'll have guests soon."

"You need support for this."

"I can handle it." She could handle anything.

"So strong." He gave her a look that said he saw right through her. "You can do it all, right?"

"Yes."

He shook his head. "No one is that strong."

"I am."

He stared at her until she felt that odd fluttering in her stomach. It annoyed her since she could see nothing in his gaze but his irritation at the worry he didn't want to feel for her.

It was ironic that once upon a time she'd wished for a prince to solve all her problems, but life had taught her the hard way that she needed to be self-reliant—at all times. She would handle this, by herself.

And besides, Cade was no prince.

"Delia—"

"Look, I don't know why you won't just drop it." She felt more desperate than ever, but her voice was sure and calm. Her voice was *always* sure and calm, thanks to years of practice.

"I can't," he said with real regret.

"Why?"

"Because I can't shake the feeling that…that you need me."

She managed to laugh at that and toss her head. "I don't need anyone, Cade, especially you."

"Yeah. I can see that." Not a man to hide his feelings for anyone, his voice was tight. She'd stirred his male pride.

In a way, Delia admired him for showing her that. With Cade, she never had to guess what he was thinking, not when his face expressed every emotion, even when he obviously didn't want to feel that emotion.

What would it be like not to worry what people thought? To just be? Delia didn't have a clue. She'd been playing at being strong and independent for so long she no longer knew how to do anything else.

"It's not a bad thing, needing someone," he said after a long moment, and because she'd often wondered about that very thing, she closed her eyes.

She thought she felt a light caress in her hair, but when she opened her eyes again, he held his reins in one hand, the other lay on his thigh.

It must have been the wind, she decided.

Cade was a man seemingly at rest. Yet power and restless energy emanated from him in waves. There was a dangerous edge to Cade McKnight, one she didn't understand. For all his casual smiles and laughter, there remained a part of him always prepared for anything. Maybe it was the bright day or the isolation, but she thought she saw a surprising depth to that edge now, and it made her take a good long look at him.

He looked back just as steadily, without a hint of discomfort.

Hurt, she realized, startled. *He was hiding a wealth of hurt,* just beneath his rough surface, and this unexpected side to the man she'd thought of only as a pain-in-her-own-rear was unsettling.

She looked away first.

The day around them was gloriously white, green, blue—a whole array of colors so brilliant that her eyes welled with stinging tears. It almost hurt to breathe, the air was so cold and crisp and pure.

So different from Los Angeles where she'd worked all her life in busy upscale beauty salons. Yes, she most definitely missed everything about it, especially the weather. Right now, she couldn't remember what fifty degrees felt like, much less seventy.

And God help her, it was only October.

But her sisters were here, she reminded herself. They loved it and she loved them. It would also be the perfect place to raise the brother she'd never known existed—if she could ever get Jacob here from Los Angeles.

That, unfortunately, depended on Cade's help. And he didn't even know it yet.

"We going to ride?" Cade asked lightly.

"Yes." She drew a deep breath and urged Betsy to walk. The stark wild land before her was the most incredible she'd ever seen, she'd give it that much. When they'd first arrived, the Triple M had been nothing more than two run-down barns and a house ready to collapse.

Over the past few months she and her sisters, along with Ty Jackson, their neighbor and now Zoe's fiancé, had worked their fingers to the bone and their bank accounts to the limit. Due to inexperience and lack of funds, they'd been forced to give up the idea of ranching. Instead, they'd opened a guest ranch.

It was harder than anything she'd ever done, and if she was in an admitting sort of mood, she'd have to say it was also the most rewarding thing she'd ever done.

Now, looking over the land they'd worked so hard on, Delia felt a fierce surge of pride for what they'd accomplished.

It was all thanks to Constance Freeman, a woman she hadn't gotten the chance to meet, but who could have been her paternal grandmother. Family.

In a shocking move, Cade came close and cupped her jaw in his leather-gloved hand, gently but firmly bringing up her chin so that she was forced to look at him. "You're a million miles away and you don't want to talk about it, right?"

"Right."

To soothe her, or maybe to combat the glare she knew she'd shot him, his thumb slid over the skin of her cheek once, then again. Her skin rippled in reaction to the touch that should have been impersonal, but wasn't.

Not even close.

With his hand on her, his eyes hot and intense, it became difficult to think, much less speak. His big body sat in the saddle as if he were born to it, his long, loose limbs at rest, but as the master of control, Delia wasn't fooled.

The darkly handsome man was battle-ready.

For her.

For some reason, that shot a pure undeniable thrill through her. *Control,* she reminded herself. She had it. Or she had, until Scott Felton, Jacob's caseworker, had informed her of the possible trouble she was in for, since the courts were happy with Jacob's current custody situation. Jacob's father had originally had custody, but then he'd died and custody had gone to Delia's mother. When she'd died as well, years later, with no will, Jacob had had to move again. He'd nearly gone into the welfare system when they'd finally located a distantly related aunt. No judge wanted to uproot the boy yet again, especially for someone Jacob didn't even know.

But Delia wanted her brother safe and sound, and with her. She thought she might know how he felt, for she'd been five years old when she'd been left in a group home. Those first years had been spent dreaming of a family taking her and making her theirs.

It hadn't happened.

Most people didn't want a little kid, they wanted a baby.

Back then, Delia had decided she didn't care. She had Zoe and Maddie, and they were more than enough.

All their lives, they'd had nothing but each other. They'd survived. Zoe had done it by being unruly and defensive, and tough when she had to be. Maddie had done it by being quiet and reserved. Accepting.

Delia had survived by masking her emotions so thoroughly that no one could see what she was feeling or thinking. She donned this protective mask every day, just as she did her makeup and clothes. It was a part of her. She needed no one, and no one needed her.

But now she had a brother—eight-year-old Jacob. He was alone, too, or had been. That gave them a kinship she couldn't ignore. Yet it went deeper than that, far deeper.

For the first time in Delia's life, she faced the truth...she *needed* to be needed by someone. Yes, she had her sisters, and yes, they loved one another with all their hearts.

But they were independent.

Jacob was too young for that. He was just a child, and needing was part of his life.

Yet whenever she called him, which had been daily, he'd been distant, reserved. She understood.

Still, protective feelings welled up. So did frustration and, yes, a good amount of bitterness and humiliation, for her mother hadn't left a will. She'd left no information about her *other* child—Delia.

She'd meant that little to her own mother.

As a result, she was last in line for Jacob now. And because of his sizable inheritance from his deceased father, the court was doubly leery of Delia's request. It didn't help that she didn't have a penny to her name. She worked sixty hours a week trying to make a success of their guest ranch, but the fact remained—she was a poor nobody.

It was natural to think of Constance's inheritance, the one Delia hadn't cared about until now. If she was owner of the Triple M...well, that would be different, right? She'd have collateral, a real job. *Importance.*

The court would have to consider her seriously then. As much as she hadn't wanted to believe it, money did make the world go around.

The wind blew, making her shiver. Reminding her that she was all too mortal. Reminding her that she was nearly twenty-six years old and still wishing for her prince to save her. He'd sure come in handy now, because no one could laugh at her if she was married to royalty. He'd be mature and kind. He'd love her above all else.

He would *not* be big and broody and tough and rugged.

He would not be rowdy and mischievous.

He would not be anything like Cade McKnight.

"I'm done riding," she said.

"You mean you're done with me."

"Nothing personal," she muttered.

Which had him letting out a grim laugh. "Like hell." But he turned his horse away without another word, almost as if he was just as eager as she to be alone.

They made it halfway back to the ranch in silence. She watched the landscape, and Cade watched her. She felt his gaze on her hair, her face. Her body.

She was used to men staring at her. Men had always stared at her since she'd hit maturity—it was a fact of life. She was five foot eight, willowy yet curvy, and blond. And yes, she supposed, beautiful.

To her, it was a curse.

But Cade's gaze was different, she had to admit. It made her feel funny, rubbery in her limbs, liquidy in parts of her anatomy she didn't usually pay attention to. And if a portion of her, a deep private portion, tingled with a strange anticipation, she could ignore it.

She was *not* attracted to him.

"I'm your friend, Delia," Cade said into their awkward silence. "Or I could be."

It was just a word—*friends*. There was no reason for her heart to tip on its side.

No reason at all.

"We're *not*. You usually ignore me, and if you don't, we can hardly stand in the same room without shooting sparks off each other."

The expression on his face made her toes curl.

"You going to deny it?" she pressed.

He let out a short almost baffled laugh as he rubbed the back of his neck. "Hell, no. Maybe I used to be able to ignore you. But then I found you crying in the kitchen. It's the funniest damn thing, but now I can't get that out of my mind. And yeah, we shoot sparks off each other, enough to light up the city of Boise with electricity for a year, and it only seems to get worse."

She nodded, satisfied.

Then he shattered that satisfaction. "But lust tends to do that."

"Who said anything about…"

"Lust?" His crooked grin was appealing enough to coax one out of a saint. "Because you do realize that's what those sparks are, right?"

"Dream on, McKnight." She pulled back on the reins and was grateful when her horse actually stopped. "This isn't about lust or even friendship."

Cade stopped his horse, as well, again with no visible sign or word. "What, then?"

"Ego."

"Ego?" He looked shocked.

"Foolish male pride. Whatever you want to call it."

He stared at her for a second, then threw back his head and laughed. The rich sound echoed around them while she gritted her teeth.

Eventually his amusement died and he sighed as he wiped away a tear of mirth. "I'm not certain what kind of jerks you were used to in L.A. But out here in the real world—" he snagged her reins and pulled her horse in close "—we do things different."

With one hand in front of her holding the leather, his other behind her bracing himself on the seat of her saddle, he leaned close. So close she could see that his eyes weren't just dark brown as she'd thought, but layered with golden specks that danced with the sunlight. So close she could smell the one-hundred-percent male scent of him.

So close she could do nothing but catch her breath and stare, feeling completely surrounded.

Held.

Good Lord, he just might be right about the lust part. "A man is a man," she managed, proud of her steady voice.

"Wrong," he whispered. "And any time you want me to show you how different some men can be…" His voice had gone husky. His gaze dipped to her mouth, made her tummy flutter again. "You just tell me."

"Never going to happen." Her voice wasn't so steady now.

He noticed and, damn him, his lips quirked. "Never say never."

She thought it would be safe to say it in this case, but she wisely kept her mouth shut.

And they rode the rest of the way back to the Triple M in complete silence.

Chapter 2

The Triple M Guest Ranch was to be open from Thursday to Sunday every week. Originally they hadn't planned to accept guests during the autumn and winter months at all, but financial problems had forced them to give it a try.

The reservations had started to trickle in, giving the sisters tentative hope of success.

The rumor was, autumn in Idaho was heaven on earth. At least that's what their brochure claimed. And for those who enjoyed the unique—and drastic—weather, it was true.

Delia didn't get it.

The spiders were huge, the air so cold it hurt to breathe and the water so soft she couldn't do a thing with her hair.

But she absolutely loved being with her sisters, loved watching them get a kick out of life for a change, and there was no denying that they loved this existence.

She'd learn to love it, too, she decided. For them. So she carried bug spray, wore lots of warm layers and kept her hair pulled back so she couldn't see it.

Now she walked through the large ranch house, which they'd worked so hard on to clean up. What a job that had been. Everything had been in a sorry state of repair when they'd first arrived last summer. With little more than the clothes on their backs, they'd been sorely challenged to make a go of it, but no one was better at surviving than Zoe, Maddie and Delia.

Delia's boots clicked on the clean but scarred wood floors. Around her, the house creaked in the wind, a happy sort of sound. She stopped at the hall telephone, thinking she'd like to call Jacob, but it was too late. Besides, one more strained phone call between them and she might break. She had to remain strong. It gave her hope.

She moved to the sliding glass door in the living room, which led to the wraparound deck. They had one week until their grand opening, and aside from the sound of the wind in the eaves, the house was quiet and peaceful.

Normally Delia loved whatever time she could grab for herself, but now she had too much time to think.

It didn't help that Cade was still on the ranch, driving her to distraction with his light teasing and hot eyes. He was nothing but a thorn in her side, but granted, he was the sexiest thorn she'd ever had. Thank God he wasn't a man to stay in one place long enough for a post office to find him. He'd be off soon, she was sure of it. That was how he was made, with a powerful wanderlust she would never understand.

He scared her, she forced herself to admit, resting her forehead against the glass and staring out into the deep dark night. He definitely scared her. After all, Delia needed no one and had made sure no one needed her. As a result, she'd bent people to her will with little to no effort. Teachers, friends. Men.

But not Cade McKnight.

He was truly his own man, one who refused to bow to any authority except his own.

It was frightening to realize she could never control a man like that. But no matter. Despite what he'd said about no longer being able to ignore her, she could still ignore him.

Needing air, regardless of how cold it was, she stepped out into the night, onto the deck that Ty had recently rebuilt. She heard bubbles, which she knew came from the newly installed hot tub, and she followed the sound in search of her sisters, seeking what only they had been able to give her.

Acceptance.

She found Zoe and Ty blissfully immersed in

the steaming water, entwined. They were kissing—
a deep passionate kiss that made Delia sigh theat-
rically even as something deep within her yearned.
"Don't you guys ever do anything other than con-
nect your mouths?"

Ty lifted his wet head and shot her a wicked
grin. "Uh-huh."

Zoe smacked him lightly on his chest and smiled
up at her sister. "Come on in, Dee. It feels terrific
on sore muscles."

Ty's grin faded. "You hurt something?"

His concern was touching...and embarrassing,
considering it was her bottom that hurt the most
from the unaccustomed riding. Zoe and Ty did
most of the physical work on the ranch, working
the horses and their small herd of cattle. Maddie
ran the kitchen, providing all meals. Delia's job
was managing the reservations and the front desk,
which included checking people in and out and
keeping up the house.

It wasn't very physical—anyone could have
done it. Which was the root of most of her guilt,
because she didn't feel she was pulling her weight.
She didn't belong and she knew that; she just
couldn't admit it to her sisters.

Ty straightened, standing in the tub, a frown
marring his brow as water dripped off his well-
built frame. He was one of the most handsome men
she'd ever seen. "What did you hurt?" he asked.

Zoe snickered and Delia sent her a dirty look.
"Nothing," she muttered.

Some of his fierceness drained, but none of his curiosity, and finally Zoe took pity on her clueless husband-to-be. "She hurt her rear end yesterday during her riding lesson." She shoved back her wet auburn hair. "She's got first-timer's butt."

"It was my *second* lesson," Delia corrected with icy dignity.

Ty bit his lip, but his eyes danced with humor. "Maybe Cade ought to take it easier on you next time."

Ty and Zoe laughed then, revoltingly disgusting in their happiness.

"Speaking of Cade, why is he still here, anyway?"

Ty lifted a brow at Delia's question, glancing at Zoe before answering. "You know he's working."

"You mean eating us out of house and home."

"Well, technically, that's Maddie's fault," Ty countered. "She's too good a cook."

"But we don't even know anything about him—his background, where he came from…anything."

Something flickered in Ty's eyes. *Knowledge of Cade,* Delia realized, and whatever it was, it wasn't pleasant.

She'd known from the first time she'd looked into Cade's dark gaze that he'd suffered in his past. But to know the details of that suffering would be to know him far more intimately than she ever intended, especially when she didn't intend to know him at all.

"Cade's past isn't important to Constance's case

or our friendship with him," Ty said carefully. "He's trustworthy and honest, and as far as I'm concerned, that's all that matters."

"He's a friend," Zoe agreed softly, reaching for Ty's hand and smiling at him with love in her eyes. "Without him we wouldn't be here."

"I know." Delia sighed, then kicked off her boots, pulled off her socks and crossed to the edge of the tub. Pulling up a chair, she sank into it, set her bare chilled feet into the water and moaned with pleasure.

Moving close, Zoe put her hand on Delia's leg. "What's the matter?"

Delia shifted away. "Nothing."

"Delia."

She sighed, rubbed her temples. *Everything,* she wanted to say. *I can't control this place. I can't control what happens to Jacob. I can't control these strange feelings I'm having for Cade.* "I don't know what's wrong." It was a half-truth. Which was as good as a lie, something she'd never told to either Zoe or Maddie.

Still standing, Ty divided a look between them. "Is this the kind of talk where men aren't invited?"

It seemed like forever that there'd been no one but Zoe and Maddie in Delia's life. But now there was Ty, too, and though Delia didn't trust men on principle, Zoe, the tough fiercely independent sister, loved him with all her heart. That made him okay in Delia's book. "You can stay."

"Good," he said with a grateful shiver, sinking back into the water. "Not just because I was starting to freeze, which I was, but because as your brother, I have to hear all the gossip or I'm completely ineffective when I tease you."

Delia narrowed her eyes. "Brother?"

"Well, yeah." He gently tugged on a lock of her hair. "Which means I get to annoy you often, you know. I also get to inspect all future boyfriends and grill them until their eyes cross. And beating up anyone who hurts you is just a given."

The strangest thing happened. Delia's heart constricted, making her chest far too tight to breathe. A warmth filled her. To cover that, and all the confusing emotions that went with it, she punched him. "I can take care of myself."

"Not with a punch like that you can't."

Zoe smiled at the banter, but still watched Delia carefully. "What's really going on, Dee? Why did you ask about Cade?"

"I just think he can solve this case from his office in Boise." *Or maybe from the other side of the country.*

"He's not…bothering you in any way, is he?" This from Ty, who Delia knew cared deeply about Cade. After all, without Cade, Ty would never have met Zoe. Or any of them for that matter.

"No, he's not bothering me," Delia said slowly. *Not much other than occupying my every single thought.* "But as my big brother, would you really beat him up for me if he was?"

"You better believe it, baby."

Zoe laughed, running her hand over her fiancé's straining biceps as he comically flexed for them. "Isn't Cade bigger than you?"

"It's not about brawn," Ty assured her, giving up the pose and laughing when Zoe rolled her eyes. "It's all in how you use it."

Zoe shook her head. "Men."

Ty kissed her laughing mouth, which made Zoe melt and Delia…well, she melted, too, but she couldn't get sidetracked. Once upon a time it had mattered greatly to Zoe who inherited the Triple M. Delia knew Zoe had wanted to be the heir with all her heart. Unfortunately it wasn't meant to be, and Zoe seemed to have come to terms with it.

Which didn't make this any easier.

Zoe pulled back from Ty. "Come on, Delia, tell me what's up."

"It's complicated."

"Well, we're pretty good at complicated," Zoe told her dryly. "Our whole life has been complicated."

Yes, but how to explain that her need to be the heir was greater than either of her sisters'? That she hated to need anything at all, but to need this, this huge thing, was nearly killing her.

"It's the investigation," Zoe guessed. "Cade's investigation for Constance."

"No."

"It's Jacob, then. Oh, honey, I wish I could make this all work out, right now."

"Me, too." This was so hard. With all her heart, she wanted happiness for Zoe and Maddie. But she also wanted Jacob. How to hurt one sibling over another?

She couldn't.

She'd have to do this on her own, have to prove her worth to the judge. She wouldn't ask her sisters for help unless it became absolutely necessary. "It's nothing," she said quietly as the weight of her lies buried her. "I'm just…tired."

"Of course you are, with all this worrying over Jacob. You talked to him today?"

"Yesterday." If one could call it that, for Jacob didn't do much other than respond to her with monosyllabic answers.

Yes, he liked school.

No, he didn't have too much homework.

Yes, he liked sports.

No, he didn't know where the Triple M was.

And given his tone, he didn't care, but there was always the slightest quiver in his voice, the smallest hesitation, and she clung to that, having to believe it *did* matter to him, that he was just uncertain and afraid.

Time, she reminded herself. He needed time.

"I know you want to go to Los Angeles alone," Zoe said. "But I wish you'd let us come with you."

Delia knew they would drop everything. They'd cancel guests, they'd spend money they didn't have. They'd do anything for her, anything at all, including hurting their future.

Delia was many things, but she refused to be that selfish. "I'll be fine."

Zoe nodded reluctantly, clearly not believing, but unwilling to push further. "Promise if you change your mind, you'll tell us. We'd be there, Delia, in a heartbeat."

"I know."

With one lithe motion, Zoe was out of the water. "I haven't seen you this upset in a long time," she said dripping water everywhere. "It scares me."

"This is upset?" Ty looked from one woman to the other. "She hasn't even raised her voice."

"Delia never raises her voice." Zoe bent to take Delia's hand, looking deeply into her eyes. "Jacob is yours, honey. The court will see that."

Delia closed her eyes.

"And as for Cade…"

Delia's eyes flew open again. *That name,* she thought darkly. Just that name altered her pulse.

"He belongs here, too."

Ty got out of the tub and wrapped his fiancée in a towel. "Let's go inside," he decided. "I'll get everyone a hot drink and we'll discuss how much Delia will pay me to kick Cade out on his tough rear end."

"We're not kicking anyone out." Zoe was still watching Delia. "Honey, you know we can't. He's a part of this family now, and when you think about it, whatever is bothering you, you'll realize we can't hurt his feelings.''

''Feelings?'' Worry and stress hardened Delia's voice. ''If he didn't have to be here, he'd be long gone, having easily forgotten all about us.''

The sound of someone male clearing his throat came from behind her. ''Well, that's flattering.'' The voice was hauntingly familiar.

Delia groaned, wished for the night to be even darker so that she could vanish. She turned and saw Cade standing there, leaning his big body against the doorjamb, his arms casually crossed over his chest. ''You must not think too highly of me,'' he said quietly, his unsmiling eyes on hers, ''if you think I could easily forget anything about you.''

It was embarrassing. Ridiculous. Silly even. But she could think of nothing to say, couldn't even find her legendary cool, so she did the only thing she could.

She grabbed her shoes, squared her shoulders and walked right past him, as well as Zoe and Ty, into the night.

And for once, she was grateful for the icy air because it cooled her heated cheeks.

But not her dreams.

Oh, she definitely has a bee in her bonnet, Cade thought as he came upon Delia on her hands and knees in the dining room the next day, scrubbing a stubborn stain on the hardwood floor.

Her hair was loose and shining, and her back-side... He took an extra-long moment to admire the way it shimmied and shaked as she worked. Her long legs were tense with strain, and for an insane moment he wished they were tense and strained...around him.

He had no idea what was running through her head, but he could safely bet his last dollar it wasn't anything close to his own lusty thoughts. "A penny for your thoughts," he ventured.

She stiffened, making him smile. God, she was so easy to rile.

"Hell," he said, grinning at her uptight pretty little spine. "I'll give you everything I have for them." Opening his wallet, he pulled out a bill. "How about five bucks?"

She sat back on her heels, wearing her queen-to-peasant expression that never failed to stir his blood.

Off-limits, McKnight, he reminded himself. *Way off limits.*

Still, egged on by some perverse need to see her ruffled out of her cool calm, he waved the money. "What do you say?"

Her lips, wide and oh-so-kissable, tightened. She looked away, but not before he caught a flash of...vulnerability? When he frowned and looked again, it was gone. Which was good. Delia wasn't vulnerable, no more than he was, well, able to set-tle down. "Hey, if anyone's upset about last night, it should be me. It was my reputation you were slandering.''

"I'm sorry," she said. "I certainly didn't mean for you to hear."

But not sorry she hurt his feelings, he noted, torn between the sting of that and humor at her fierce pride.

She was so in control.

He wondered what it would take to have the city girl lose the reins on that tightly held control. He couldn't help the possibilities that tumbled through his head, starting with a hot deep wet kiss. Yeah, that would do it nicely. He could picture it—her long blond hair falling around him, brushing his bare belly, his thighs. Her lush lips would curve gently, her eyes molten as she softened with desire.

But Delia wasn't soft at all. She was staring at him, her frosty-blue eyes narrowed, her body taut as a bow.

He should walk away.

And yet he couldn't. He'd known the three of them, Zoe, Maddie and Delia, for far too long to do that now. In spite of himself and his past, he'd grown to care for them, felt responsible for them coming so far from their home city of Los Angeles to the wilds of Idaho.

But it was more than that, and though he wasn't willing to name it, Delia seemed to be at the bottom of it. He hardly knew her, he understood that. She had a knack for hiding her true self, for being incredibly stingy with emotions. He understood that, too. Though he hated it, it made him all the more curious, and there was nothing worse than a curious investigator.

In spite of needing to be far away from here and from this woman who drew him as no other had in too long, he worried about her. "You seem uptight today."

"I thought I was always uptight."

"Well, there's uptight and then there's *uptight*."

"I'm fine."

But she wasn't, for whatever reason, and he knew it. He'd known it the other night when he'd found her in the dark in the kitchen, with tears in her huge blue eyes.

He had other cases to be obsessing over, had a whole other life, in fact, and yet the Triple M haunted him.

Delia haunted him.

She was staring down at her cleaning supplies as if they held the greatest interest.

Cade knew his instincts were razor sharp. They'd saved his life more times than he could count, and they were screaming now. "Ownership of this place would be incredible," he said carefully, seemingly out of the blue, but he'd had a hunch.

She flinched before she could control it, confirming his guess.

Bingo. "You know I'm doing my damnedest to get proof of that ownership," he said softly. "Whether it turns out to be you or Maddie."

"I know."

He tried a different tack. "Your father—tell me about him."

"I have an idea." She'd risen and now grabbed her broom and started sweeping. "Let's talk about you, instead," she said.

"Me? Why?"

"Because you're one big mystery."

"My past isn't relevant to this case."

"And therefore doesn't need to be discussed?"

"Exactly. Now tell me about your father."

"You're a hard man, Cade McKnight."

"From you, Delia, I take that as a compliment." He was surprised when she smiled. "Your father?" he repeated patiently.

"You mean, could he have been Ethan Freeman?" She'd given up trying to get information out of him, whether because it wasn't important to her, or because she knew he wasn't about to indulge her curiosity, he had no clue.

"We've already discussed this," she said, leaning on her broom. "All I ever knew was what my mother told me when I was five, just before she took me to the foster home."

And had left her there, without a word. What kind of mother, Cade wondered, would just dump her child like that? He came from a large loving family of six. His mother would no more give up a child than her own right arm. And even when Cade had walked away from that family, his heart destroyed, she'd never turned her back on him, instead, had badgered and badgered until he'd come back to the fold.

Delia set aside the broom and lifted one of the three windows. Immediately a cool breeze hit them. Delia's sweater plastered itself to her lush form. Cade tried not to look, he really did, but she was so beautiful.

And remote.

"She said he was an undercover cop on assignment," Delia continued in that low husky voice, the one that screamed sex.

Or maybe it was just his own mind that screamed sex. "Undercover cop," he repeated, shaking his head to clear it.

"Top-secret assignment. I don't think she even told him I existed."

Cade had taken on some heartbreaking cases before, not to mention his own unspeakable heartbreak. He prided himself on his ability to harden himself, separate himself from any pain, his own or his clients.

But he didn't seem to be able to do that with Delia, and it disturbed him that he felt her anguish as his own. In fact, it multiplied his own. "We know Ethan Freeman disappeared about that time."

"Just as we know it's unlikely he became a cop," she countered. "So unless you've missed something or made a mistake…"

It was possible. God knew, he'd certainly made

plenty of mistakes in his life. His biggest had cost the lives of the two people he'd cared about most.

Delia stared sightlessly out the window, showing more emotion in just her weary stance than Cade had ever seen her show.

"The three of you are sharing the ranch no matter who inherits," he said.

"Yes, we knew we would do that before we even got here."

"Then why does it matter which of the three of you actually owns the Triple M?"

It took her a second longer than usual, but her eyes shuttered and she drew herself up. "You couldn't possibly understand, not with your life-style."

Since she knew nothing about his life-style or why he led it, that shouldn't have hurt.

"And, anyway, it matters," she whispered.

Cade knew how close she and her sisters were, knew that they had clung together out of a need for more than mere survival during their childhood years. They'd been mother, father, sibling and best friend to one another. They'd been one another's sole support. Out of that had grown a deep abiding love that was stronger than in most blood-related families.

Despite himself, despite how many years it had been, something deep and frozen in Cade cracked. Thawed. He'd had a family once.

A wife and a beautiful son.

But Lisa and Tommy were dead, had been for eight long years now.

As a result, he lived for his cases, as wide and diversified as he could get them and as scattered across the globe as possible. It helped bury his pain, the all-consuming pain that was too great to think about. Actually, it was far easier not to think at all, instead, taking on case after case, working himself half to death, pushing himself to the very limit and then beyond, so he could fall into bed at night so exhausted he couldn't even dream. Traveling was a way of life for him, the only way, because if he stayed in one spot too long he lost himself.

It was that simple.

He'd been on this case too long, and the wanderlust part of him was raging to run far and never look back at this place, which was beginning to feel too much like a home.

Damn. Not that. Not ever again did he want a home, a warm safe place that could only, in the end, hurt him. Soon enough he'd solve this case and be on his way, he promised himself. And until then, he'd be an idiot to encourage any more ties than absolutely necessary.

But Delia blew out a harsh breath. "I need to be heir to get Jacob."

Don't ask. Just back off, McKnight. "Jacob is your brother," he said, instead. "I'm betting the court rules in your favor."

"The court is going to snub its nose at me."

Her voice was clear enough, but her hands shook when she again reached for the broom.

And despite all his talk about no ties and distance, he moved closer. "What are you talking about? Of course they won't."

"I'm financially insolvent, I'm a thousand miles away from Jacob's home, and I'm single. I'm not exactly parenting material."

He thought that was pretty much crap and said so.

Her lips tightened, but it was as if the veil of control lifted for that one second, and he suddenly saw the truth.

She didn't believe herself worthy.

Distance. Lord, he sorely needed it, but there was none coming, not when she was standing there pretending to be so strong and fierce when inside she was incredibly vulnerable, so much so that he ached to hold her. "Delia...you'll get him."

She just shrugged.

He was leaving Idaho soon. *Wanted* to be leaving. *Couldn't wait to be leaving.*

So why, then, did his heart contract just from looking at her struggling with pride, rigid with the effort to be strong for everyone?

Who was strong for her?

"You're leaving for Los Angeles in a few days," he said slowly. "To meet Jacob."

"Yes."

"I have a case there. I could come with you, try to help—"

"No," she said quickly. "I'll do this alone."

He watched her gather her supplies, watched her move away from him, and with everything he had, he wanted to let it go. Wanted to let *her* go.

"Hell," he muttered, knowing he couldn't let her go alone. Knowing also that it was far more than mere friendly concern.

Chapter 3

Delia got on the plane, found her window seat, then buckled in and straightened her skirt to avoid wrinkles.

First impressions were everything, and she intended to make a good one on Scott Felton, Jacob's social worker. He'd known Jacob for six years, ever since Jacob's father had died. He was close to Jacob, perhaps closer than anyone at this point, and his approval or nonapproval could make or break her case.

"Excuse me, dear." An elderly woman stood in the aisle, wearing eye-popping chartreuse sweats, high-top tennis shoes and a ski cap.

Delia willed her to keep moving—not that she had anything against old women, but this one looked like a talker and it was a long flight.

"Sadie," the woman informed Delia, as if she'd asked for her name. "Sadie Walkins. Howdy." Her arms were completely loaded and she proceeded to stuff the overhead bin with two large shopping bags. Then she plopped into the middle seat, directly next to Delia, and smiled.

"Whew, those things are darned heavy. It's no wonder they wanted me to check them. I refused, though, because I like to keep my stuff with me, don't you? Though I have to say, I don't think they're too happy with me about now." Pushing at the glasses slipping down her nose, the woman shifted around, bumping Delia's arms and legs until at last she was apparently comfortable. "Oh, aren't you lovely?" she said to Delia, staring at her.

"Thank you," Delia murmured. She didn't have to glance in a mirror or notice the looks she'd been getting from the male passengers to know she looked good. The woman who'd taken her ticket had complimented her on her outfit, and Delia knew she'd have been shocked to know it was handmade. Nearly every stitch of clothing Delia owned had been made with her own hands. It was a throwback to the years she and her sisters had gone without enough money for anything as frivolous as clothes, but somewhere along the line she'd learned to love the freedom of designing and sewing her own stuff, anyway.

Yet it wasn't the woman next to her she wanted

to impress, but the man who was standing in the way of her future with Jacob.

Maybe she should have worn a suit. A power suit, her great little red one...

God, she hated this all-encompassing fear of not being good enough, because that was exactly what this silly obsessing about her clothes came down to—her inadequacy and the certainty that Scott would see it.

"I'm going to visit my grandkids," Sadie offered next. "Though why anyone would want to live in Los Angeles is beyond me."

Delia loved Los Angeles, so she didn't respond and just stared out the window. Jacob lived there. He was a city boy, too, how would he feel about the Triple M?

Idaho and its distinct majestic landscape stared back at her, silent.

"It's so...dirty," Sadie said. "Filth."

All Delia had ever known was the hustling, bustling, teeming, crowded, glorious Los Angeles. She hadn't been back since they'd left early last summer, and she wondered if it was as wonderful as she remembered. The people, the sights, the smells...yeah, it would be the same.

But was she?

Sighing, she leaned back and closed her eyes.

"Excuse me," came a deep male voice. "Can I get you anything?"

What? They hadn't even taken off yet, and it wasn't as if she sat in first class—

Wait. She knew that voice.

Opening her eyes she looked over Sadie's head and into the grinning gaze of Cade McKnight. *"You,"* she said.

He winked. "Me."

He stood there as if he didn't have a care in the world, looking annoyingly good, smiling easily and effortlessly, altering her pulse. He wore khaki pants and a soft-looking white shirt unbuttoned at the collar. His dark hair fell to that collar in reckless waves that Delia imagined a less-disciplined woman would have a hard time keeping her fingers off.

Good thing she was especially disciplined. Still, from deep inside her came a strong tingling, which she ruthlessly told herself must be hunger because she'd skipped breakfast again. It had nothing, absolutely nothing, do to with the tall rangy wanderlust-driven man standing there. "Go home, Cade."

"Ah, but you assume I'm here for you."

That actually made her blush, because of course, he was right. She had a feeling Cade was always right. "You're flying to Los Angeles for your business?"

"Yes."

So what, then, was that undeniable intensity beneath his casual charm? An intensity aimed at her. "Go home, Cade. Wherever that may be."

"You know I can't."

"Of course you can. You just turn around and—"

"Is this your fiancé?" the older woman asked Delia, watching with delight as the too-big Cade tried to squeeze himself against the seat to let others by, his broad shoulders hunched, one long leg bent at an awkward position. He apologized to each and every person forced to pass him, but he didn't budge.

"Oh, how sweet and polite he is," Sadie said. "And so handsome. What a catch, my dear."

Some catch. The man might be a full-time private investigator, but he suffered from the strongest sense of restlessness she'd ever seen. He globe-hopped from case to case and loved it, which Delia, to whom roots and home meant everything, couldn't imagine. Zoe said he was gorgeous enough for a woman to forget such inconveniences, but gorgeous didn't count for much in Delia's book. "He's not my—"

"Men are so much handsomer now than in my day," Sadie announced, adjusting her ski cap.

From overhead came the drone of the stewardess's voice, reminding them this was a full plane. Everyone was asked to please take their seats.

With an obedience that made Delia narrow her eyes—she had a feeling he never followed the rules unless they suited him—Cade slipped into the still-empty aisle seat, and smiled with innocent charm at Sadie.

"Hello," she said, smiling back. "I'm going to visit my grandkids in Los Angeles. It's a terrible town, but what is one to do?"

"Families. Can't do much with them, can you?" he asked gently, and she beamed.

"I've told my kids to move, but do they listen to me? No."

"That's a shame." Cade shook his head. "You look like a sensible woman to me—they should listen. Now that woman next to you, she's not so sensible."

"But you're going to marry her, anyway, and take care of her." Sadie sighed dramatically. "That's so romantic."

Delia gritted her teeth at the two of them so casually discussing her, then leaned forward to glare at Cade. "He's not my—"

"When's the wedding?"

"Soon as we can manage." Cade lowered his voice to a conspiratorial whisper. "We're in a hurry, our love just can't be contained. We can't wait to—"

"*What* are you doing here?" Delia asked through a tightly clenched jaw. "And how fast can you go back to where you came from?"

Cade shot her a mock frown. "What kind of way is that to greet your fiancé?"

Delia gave up with a groan and closed her eyes.

She heard whispering, then felt shifting, and when she opened her eyes again, Cade was in the seat right next to her, his arm and thigh brushing hers. She could feel the heat of him through their clothes, and the strength he carefully held in check.

And when her gaze lifted to meet his, all traces

of amusement had been replaced by a passion she found harder to deal with than his teasing. "Cade—"

"Your light was on all night and you left at the crack of dawn," he said quietly. "You didn't sleep, you didn't eat. You can't travel like this."

"I can get by on very little sleep, and believe me, my figure could do without a meal now and then. And coming from the consummate traveler, this conversation is very strange."

"Everyone needs sleep, your body is amazing just the way it is and needs its fuel, and as a consummate traveler, I know what you're doing. You're nervous, you're uptight and you need a friend."

"Is that what you are? A friend?"

"I already told you that."

"People tell me a lot of things."

"That they don't mean?" He shook his head, never taking his gaze off hers. "Not me."

Of course she didn't believe him; it would be ridiculous to do so. But she was breathless, and she told herself it was the pressure, since the plane had started its taxi down the runway.

It had absolutely nothing to do with his thinking her body was amazing. "You should have gone home, Cade."

"Home?" The word rolled off his tongue as if it was foreign to him.

Which just proved her point. He could never really understand her and all that she held dear.

"Home. Your office in Boise. Unless you have another home, which of course, since you never say a word about yourself or your private life, I wouldn't know."

"And that disturbs you."

"I'm curious about you," she admitted. "I don't even know if you're married."

"I'm not," he said with sudden grimness. "And I don't talk about me. Ever."

So much for their friendship. "Fine. Then go. Go far away."

"Just go? Where? Anywhere, as long as it's far from you?"

"Well…yes."

He sighed. "You're a tough nut, Delia, I'll give you that. But I'm tougher."

"What does that mean?" But she knew, and let out a groan. "You're sticking."

"Like glue."

"I don't need you."

"So you've said."

"I don't want you."

His full lips curved, and his expression lightened with genuine humor. "Now, now. Let's not lie, not among friends."

"We're not friends. And I'm not lying!"

"Uh-huh."

She closed her eyes and leaned back, deciding the only way to deal with this was to ignore him.

"Dream of me," he whispered.

And damn him, she did.

* * *

The sunny warm weather in Southern California was so different from the cold autumn she'd just left, Delia couldn't believe it. How could she have forgotten, even for a moment, how delicious the weather was at all times in Los Angeles?

She rented a car from the airport, still trying to ignore Cade, which was becoming increasingly difficult, especially since each long assessing glance he gave her seemed to affect her accumulatively, so that she was aware of little else. It got so she didn't have to be looking at him; she could *feel* his every move.

Jacob, she reminded herself. Concentrate on Jacob. There had to be a way to ensure custody, which she wanted so very much. It wasn't just that she couldn't imagine letting him live anywhere else when his family was in Idaho, but also that she already loved him and had from the moment she knew he existed.

''It'll work out,'' Cade said into the silence, his voice gentle and subdued, all joking gone. ''Getting Jacob.''

Startled, she glanced at him. He was driving— he'd insisted, claiming that it would leave her mind free to race around if she wanted—and was concentrating on the road in front of him. He had the window down, his hair whipping wild in the breeze. With his sleeves shoved up to his elbows, revealing strong tanned forearms and big sure hands, he seemed relaxed. Confident. And just a tad cocky.

"How do you do that?" she asked.

"Do what?" he said innocently.

"Am I such an open book that you can read my mind?"

He risked a quick glance at her. "On the contrary, actually." He gave a smile that might have been a killer, if she wasn't immune to such things. "But I do have an edge."

"An edge?"

"Yeah. I understand you."

"That's interesting, considering we're polar opposites."

"Opposites attract," he said so grimly she realized for the first time that he resented their strange chemistry even more than she did.

Because that gave her too much to think about, she made a disagreeing sound, turned away to look out the passenger window and tried to think about other things.

Soon she'd meet her brother for the first time. Her stomach danced with jittery butterflies. What would he be like?

What would great-aunt Edna be like? It hadn't been until after their mother's death just months ago that Jacob had even met Edna. She was Delia's mother's second aunt by marriage and until last year had lived in France—which was why twenty years ago, when Delia's mother had left her in the foster home, there hadn't been anyone available to help.

Jacob must be terrified; she'd certainly been all

those years back. But in spite of everything, Delia considered herself lucky. She had found Zoe and Maddie, and they'd turned out to be her heart and soul.

Jacob had no one but Edna, and no matter how sweet and kind and wonderful she might be, it wasn't the same as close family.

Delia didn't fool herself. Getting close to Jacob—given the terse restrained phone conversations they'd had—wasn't going to be easy. But she knew what it was like to hide behind a cool facade; she'd find a way to Jacob's heart. She'd never abandon him.

But as she gave Cade the directions she'd been given, they went from the relative slums surrounding the airport to the elegant mansions of San Marino, and any confidence she'd managed to muster faded.

Jacob was living like a king.

How could she compare?

That was simple enough—she couldn't. With a sinking feeling, she stared at the house they'd pulled up in front of. Three stories of brick and windows shaped into the most charming Tudorstyle home she'd ever seen. The circular drive was surrounded with meticulous gardens, and a BMW sat in the drive, beneath a colorful flag waving the words Welcome, Friends.

She felt every bit the misplaced unwanted city girl. She couldn't do this, couldn't compete, and all her buried feelings of worthlessness worked to the surface.

At the touch on her arm, she looked into Cade's unsmiling face. Yet she had no trouble detecting the warmth and compassion that made her want to crawl into a hole.

Where was her own inner strength?

"Delia."

Instead of hugging her, as she knew he would have Zoe or Maddie, he reached over and gave her a gentle shake. "Don't you give up. You're better than that."

"In case you missed it, that little flag over there is worth more than I am."

"I'm not talking about your checkbook," he said, his disappointment in her clear. "I'm talking heart. Soul. Now get out and go show them what you're made of."

Delia stared at him as panic raced through her veins like wildfire.

"Go," he repeated firmly. "I'll wait right here."

What had she expected—him to hold her hand? She didn't need that, or him. She could do this. Drawing upon years of experience, she took a deep supposedly calming breath and got out of the car.

She might not know exactly what to do or how to reach Jacob, but she'd find a way. By herself.

Just as always.

"Delia."

She looked at Cade, bracing herself for either anger or pity.

"I believe in you," he said softly, making her heart pound ridiculously. She ignored it and walked toward the house.

Edna greeted Delia with a cool sophistication that matched her home, but the woman's eyes were warm and joyful, which gave Delia even more to worry about.

For the first time she wondered what she was trying to take Jacob away from. And did she even have that right?

Edna, with her height and undeniably regal presence, was a well-preserved sixty-eight, which Delia knew only because Edna mentioned her age as they walked through the house to the back deck. They sat at a cozy patio table laden with snacks that made Delia's empty stomach grumble loudly.

"Scott Felton will be here shortly," Edna said, which surprised Delia because the social worker had made it clear he would be present for every moment of this first meeting.

At Delia's unspoken question, something flickered across Edna's face, something that looked suspiciously like guilt. "I might have led him to believe our meeting was for half an hour from now," she said evenly.

"Might have?"

"Well…yes." There was no disguising that flash of emotion now, though it was more good humor than remorse. "I wanted to see you for myself first," Edna admitted

Delia, who could act cool, calm and collected with the best of them, didn't move, didn't so much as give a hint of her nerves and fear and worry. "And?"

"And…I like what I see." With that, she sent Delia a genuine smile. "It's funny, I never thought I'd find myself a parent, especially at my age." She waited a beat. "But I have to say, there's nothing quite as exhilarating—or as tiring—as a child."

Much as Delia wanted to meet her brother, she needed to feel out this situation. "You enjoy having him? He's happy here?"

"Yes to the first question, but as for the second, I haven't a clue." Edna sighed. "He's eight years old, he's been alone too long, neglected too long, and he's a boy. Therefore he's a master at hiding his feelings."

An unfortunate family trait, Delia thought.

"When I found out about you," Edna continued, casually pouring tea from a pot that looked like an heirloom, "I of course had you investigated."

"You what?"

"You want custody and I had to be sure that if the courts decided he should be with you, instead of any alternatives, that you would be good for him."

"Alternatives? You didn't intend to keep him?"

"I'm willing, but I'm far too old for the boy.

He won't be happy here for long." She set down her teacup and looked into Delia's eyes. "He's practically a baby, and I don't take this responsibility lightly. I had to make sure you would take care of him the way he deserves to be taken care of. The way he hasn't been taken care of until now."

Delia's heart all but stopped. "He was abused?"

"Not physically, no. But both his parents are dead, and even though they apparently didn't do much more than feed and clothe him, they were his parents. They were all he knew."

Delia thought she'd gladly go after each and every person who'd ever hurt him. She had so much to give him, so much she wanted to tell him—

"You don't look anything like me."

Delia turned toward the small voice. Standing there, glaring at her with all his eight-year-old hurting self, as if she'd personally caused all his misery, was her brother. Jacob.

He was right, they didn't look alike. She had light blue eyes and his were so dark they looked black. Her facial features were narrow and his were round, though his body was all bony angles. Her hair was blond and his was dark and disheveled. In direct contrast to that, and the scowl on his face, his clothes were neat and clean, as if he'd dressed for her visit.

She swallowed past the lump in her throat. "No, we don't look alike, do we," she agreed quietly.

"But I am your sister, and I'm very happy to meet you."

His narrow shoulders hunched. "Why?"

Stunned, Delia glanced at Edna, who merely lifted a brow and remained silent. "I'm happy," she said, turning back to the sullen little boy, "because I've always wanted more family."

"I don't know you. You're not my family."

As he spoke, his voice broke, and something inside Delia broke, as well. Rising, she moved close to the boy and hunkered down before him, not daring to touch him, though she wanted to so badly her hands shook. "I know it's scary, but we are family. I want to get to know you."

He backed up a step, coming in contact with the doorjamb. Delia reached out a hand, but with his eyes suspiciously bright, he whirled and ran off. She watched him go, her chest tight and aching.

She'd failed.

"It'll get easier," Edna said softly after a moment. "Each time it will get easier."

Delia stared at the empty doorway, willing her spinning emotions into check, fiercely blinking against the tears she adamantly refused to shed. Nothing had ever come easy for her. Nothing. It seemed this wouldn't, either. But she could do it. She could reach him.

Chapter 4

Delia tried everything, but Jacob refused to come out of his room. As kind and patient as Edna was, she refused to make him.

Scott arrived, and he was everything his voice had promised on the phone: reserved, confident and direct. Delia was as tall as he was, something she sensed irked him. He had sun-kissed blond hair, cool assessing eyes and a definite opinion on Jacob. "He's been through a lot," he said after listening to how the meeting had gone. "We need to let him adjust slowly."

Delia bit her tongue because she knew this man was her link to the courts. He had influence there, as well as with Jacob, since the two of them had developed a friendship.

"Jacob, buddy," Scott called through the door, knocking twice.

"You came!"

The joy in the little boy's voice was clear to all, and Scott beamed. He leaned closer to the door. "Ready for that pizza I promised you?"

"Yeah!" A hesitation. "We're going alone, right?"

Scott glanced at Delia. "How about we invite your sister?"

"Why?"

"Because she came a long way just to see you."

"She never wanted to see me before."

"We talked about this, Jacob," Scott said gently, still through the door. "She didn't know about you before."

"Well, I don't want to know her now."

Scott gestured for Delia to move with him away from the door so they couldn't be overheard. "He's scared," he murmured.

Delia stared longingly at the closed door. Frustration filled her. "I was hoping to spend some time with him today and tomorrow morning. I can only stay until tomorrow afternoon—I have to get back for the grand opening of our guest ranch."

Scott was silent at that, but she felt his disapproval. *Isn't Jacob more important than your guest ranch?* his eyes seemed to ask.

Of course Jacob was, but without the guest ranch, Delia would have no way to support herself, much less her brother. It was their security, their future, and she had to protect that, as well. "I'm not giving up," she told Scott, determined. "I'm coming for pizza."

"That's fine, but I'm not sure it's wise to push right now."

Well, right now was all she had. "I'll meet you there to give him a few minutes, if you'll just tell me where."

As she said her goodbyes to Edna, the older woman grasped her hand and looked deeply into her eyes. "Time," she said softly. "It'll all work out in time."

Delia wanted to point out that she didn't have much time. She'd set the wheels in motion for a custody hearing, and while she was thankful Edna didn't seem resentful but willing to go along with whatever the court decided, Delia knew the entire thing hinged on Jacob and his needs.

If only he needed her. It was pathetic to think of it that way, but Delia was nothing if not brutally honest, especially with herself.

In her entire life, not once had she ever been truly needed.

Well, too bad, she told herself. She'd survived this long—she'd be fine. It was Jacob she had to worry about, not herself.

Scott stopped her in the hallway. "You're disappointed."

"Yes," she admitted. "I knew it would be difficult, but…"

His smile was sympathetic. "But not this difficult. Jacob's got some things to work out. I think I can help him.''

''You're good with him.''

His eyes warmed. ''Yes. I…I'm very attached to him. I shouldn't say this, but he's my favorite. I care about him very much.''

''And?'' Delia paused. ''I'm sure I heard one at the end of that sentence.''

''And—'' his smile faded ''—I know you don't want to hear this, but I think it's wrong to rush him. To rush this reunion.''

''It's not a reunion, since we've never met before today, and you're right, I don't want to hear it.''

Although she'd said it in a light tone, Scott stiffened. His eyes hardened. ''I take my job very seriously, Ms. Scanlon. If I don't like what I see between you and Jacob, I'll make sure it's in my report. And that report goes to the judge to be evaluated before his final decision.''

Maybe it was the lack of sleep or the skipping of meals, or maybe it was the undeniable threat in Scott's voice, but the blood pounded in her ears. Her vision shimmered. And as it had all her life, the threat of confrontation put her chin up and temper out.

Cool as a cucumber, she smiled. ''Jacob's my brother. We're related by blood. Yes, he's upset and frightened, but once I get past that, he'll come around. And you'll see between us exactly what should be between family members. Affection. Warmth. Love.''

''I'm not the enemy here,'' Scott said. ''But if there has to be sides, I'm on Jacob's.''

''That makes two of us.'' Head high, she went out the front door. She was hurt, scared and furious. None of these showed.

She blinked in the bright California sunshine and took a deep, shaky breath.

What was she going to do? She had a brother who wouldn't acknowledge her and a social worker with an attitude. She glanced back at the huge house. Had she really thought the monetary difference between Edna and her would be her biggest obstacle?

Money had nothing to do with it.

Jacob was just scared, she told herself. And thought himself alone in that. He wasn't, whether he knew it or not.

And at the thought, a very small bit of her anxiety slipped away. No, it hadn't been the warm open-armed welcome she'd imagined, not even close, but she'd seen him, she'd looked into his dark troubled eyes and had recognized a kindred spirit.

That, and all her hopes and dreams, would have to get her through.

''Delia.''

Jolted out of her musings by Cade's husky voice, Delia came to a stop beside the rental car.

He was leaning against the driver's door, arms and ankles crossed.

A casual pose. Not such a casual man.

The sun was behind him, like a halo over his dark hair, shadowing his expression. But just the sight of him, waiting for her, did something strange to her insides.

She wasn't a woman easily affected by a man. There'd been few in her life she'd ever trusted, few she'd let know her, and fewer still who could trip her pulse.

Yet this man did exactly that and more, which didn't sit well with her. He was the opposite of everything she'd ever wanted. Security. Safety. And that other, that illusive thing she'd just today discovered about herself—that inexplicable need to be needed.

Tall, dark and tempting as he was, Cade could give her none of that.

"How did it go?" he asked, concern evident in every tense muscle.

She really hadn't had much chance to think about him and why he'd come. She'd been far too nervous and anxious about Jacob. Now she wondered what he was thinking and why she cared so much.

"Hey." Frowning, he straightened away from the car. "You okay?"

No. No, she wasn't okay. Wasn't sure when she would be okay. "I..." Suddenly being in front of Edna's house, with Scott probably watching her out the window, weighing her every move and planning her future around it, felt oppressing. "I need to get out of here," she murmured as her headache kicked in. She rubbed her temples. "Can we..."

"Yep." With surprising gentleness, he steered her around the car and opened the door for her. She expected to be grilled, but he didn't say a word, and she was grateful. "Here's the address Scott gave me," she said, handing him a slip of paper. "It's where they're going to go eat."

"Do we have some time?"

"A little, maybe." The pounding in her head made her dizzy, so she leaned back and closed her eyes. She heard the engine come on, but she didn't move. It felt good just to drift.

She must have fallen asleep because when the engine stopped, she jolted awake. They were at a park. "What...?"

"You looked like you needed a minute first, and we never talked about which hotel—"

"Hotel," she repeated inanely. God, tonight. Sleeping. And Cade, his rough and tough body sprawled restlessly between the sheets. They'd probably be tangled around him, for she didn't imagine he slept quietly.

He gave a low and sexy chuckle. "Don't you have enough to worry about without adding anything else?" he asked.

"Yes, I—"

"Tell me how it went with Jacob."

The quick change of subject, from teasing to seriousness, left her head spinning all the more. "It didn't go very well," she murmured. "In fact, I think it's safe to say it went very badly."

With amazing tenderness—she never imagined Cade could be tender—he reached up and pulled her fingers away from her temples.

"Hush," he whispered, then slipped his own fingers through her hair and massaged her head.

The moan slipped out of her before she could stop it, which horrified her. "Shh," he said, and continued to work magic with his fingers.

The windows were down. Around them were tall aspens, weaving in the light wind. The sun was warm. Children played in the distance, and birds and insects serenaded them. It was a lovely day, a lovely moment with his talented hands on her, and Delia began to relax.

"I blew it," she said. "I tried to rush Jacob when all I wanted to do was reach him. It was a fiasco."

"You'll try again."

"How?"

"You giving up already?"

Her gaze whipped to his, registered the direct challenge there, and within a second her self-pity ceased. "Do I look like a quitter, McKnight?"

His lips curved slowly as his gaze ran over her, lingering in spots that suddenly tingled, making her heart dance that funny little dance again. "No, ma'am,'' he drawled. "You certainly don't look like a quitter to me.''

Darn it, but that smile of his was a lethal weapon. "Tell me again why you're here. With me. And don't give me the friend thing again. It doesn't fly.''

"No?'' In the blink of an eye he was closer, so much so that she could feel his warm breath on her face. "Let's try this, then.''

And his mouth came down on hers.

She made a noise that Cade took to mean she was surprised, but hell, that made them even. He hadn't meant to kiss her, but he did, and she tasted like heaven. Because he wanted more, he nibbled at her lips until she let him deepen the kiss. Now *he* made the noise of surprise because something happened, something really good. An almost forgotten sense of wicked abandon came over him.

As his hands swept up and down her arms, she shivered, making that little sound again, the one that reminded him of a kitten getting its belly rubbed. He decided he liked that sound a lot.

She clung to him, her fingers tangled in his hair as she held his head close, but he was so breathless from just that one kiss he tore his mouth from hers and buried his face in her neck. He found skin so sweet and soft he had to explore it with his tongue. Then the sensitive spot beneath her ear drew him, and he kissed her there.

She whispered his name on a sigh, making herself vulnerable in a way he hadn't imagined this strong woman ever doing.

It was startling, shocking, humbling.

So was how much he wanted her.

Rocked to the core, Cade leaned back just enough to see her face. His shock was mirrored right back at him, and more. There was stunned arousal, too. And fear.

That had been no ordinary kiss, in fact, that had been like no other kiss he'd ever had.

Delia's breath came in uneven little pants, and her lush mouth was still wet and now slightly swollen. Clearly she was in no better shape than he to examine what had just happened and why.

"Time for pizza?" he asked, his voice gravelly with desire.

"Yes!" she agreed quickly. "Yes." Backing away, she adjusted her seat belt, ran a hand through her hair, anything to avoid meeting his eyes. But that was okay with Cade because he knew what was in his eyes—a mixture of confusion and lust, and he sure as hell wasn't ready to face either. Not with this woman, the one woman in far too long who seemed able to saunter right past his defenses directly to his heart.

Switching on the ignition, he drove out of the quiet park and back into the real world, where he was just the private investigator on a case that would soon be over, and she was just a client. Where neither of them would be tempted again because they were wrong for each other, all wrong.

* * *

Wrong for each other, he reminded himself at the pizza parlor where he watched Delia try to win the approval of a brother who wasn't going to be easily reached.

Wrong for each other, he reminded himself again on the drive to the hotel she'd chosen when it was all he could do to concentrate on the road, when he really wanted to snag the too-quiet Delia close for an embrace he was sure wouldn't be entirely for comfort.

Wrong for each other, he reminded himself yet again when they got to the hotel and their separate rooms, and Delia disappeared into hers, her willowy body slow with exhaustion, her eyes shadowed and troubled.

Suddenly it hit him right there and then, with the force of a tornado, as he stood there in the hallway of the hotel holding his key in one hand and his heart in the other, ready to be crushed. Again.

He was starting to fall.

It wouldn't, couldn't happen. First of all, with the exception of that one amazing kiss, she didn't want him. She wanted someone who could give her a home, a future. Love.

He couldn't do any of that.

He didn't want a home, not ever again. It was bad enough he'd been stuck out on the ranch for as long as he had with his case. No, what he needed was to get out, to be free without any restraints, and he needed this with a violent urgency he nearly couldn't contain.

He had other cases, he reminded himself. Plenty of them. And all along, when the coziness and warmth of the Triple M had gotten too much for him, when it reminded him of things better left in his past, he'd used those cases to run.

But he'd always come back.

He was going to have to remedy that.

Easier said than done, because that night, when he could have been working or reading or even sleeping, he lay in bed in his lonely hotel room and studied the ceiling. Thinking.

Yearning. Aching.

Watching Delia tonight had been heartbreaking.

Jacob was a small kid, but with eyes as sharp as a tack. He didn't miss much, and certainly not the fact that Delia was trying to please both him and Scott.

Jacob had weaseled a shocking amount of quarters out of her, then managed to snub her when she offered to play some of the games with him, instead choosing Scott, who'd looked delighted at the invitation.

Unintentional or not, Scott hadn't helped matters any, because his mere presence made it easy for Jacob to ignore Delia.

Cade figured all Jacob needed was to be told Delia was his sister and that was that. Family was family. The kid was decent, but he was wary and afraid, almost as if he needed to give himself permission to accept Delia.

Cade had wanted to do that for her, to slam his hands on the table and tell Jacob to listen up and face facts. He'd wanted...to act like a father.

Wasn't *that* a joke. He'd had his one shot at being a father, a husband, too. His family had loved him in spite of all his faults, and he'd returned that love with all his unscarred heart. But he'd failed them, and because of that, had caused their deaths, no matter how inadvertently.

Wouldn't everyone who knew him now be shocked to know that? Shocked to know he did everything in his power to not think about it? That he used his job to hide from his past?

Yeah, maybe thinking about the hauntingly beautiful Delia helped a little, helped him forget his weaknesses, but he didn't deserve that. He didn't deserve a second shot at happiness.

Ever.

Chapter 5

"The house looks perfect, Delia. You really out-did yourself." Maddie smiled as she came into the front room, which would serve as the living room and reception area for their guests.

Delia looked around at the old but polished wood floors, at the antique furniture they'd hauled down from the attic and cleaned, at the huge picture windows that so perfectly showcased the mountains in the distance.

"I didn't get that highest window clean enough," Delia murmured, seeing a smudge nearly twelve feet up, close to the open-beam ceilings. "I just need to get a ladder and—"

"And nothing," Maddie said firmly, coming closer. "Honey, you've been working for two days solid, ten hours a day, ever since you got back from L.A. You can't keep up this pace. You're going to get sick.''

"Hard work never hurt anyone. But that window—''

"Is far more fine than you. You're exhausted.''

"I'm just going to—''

"Take a break,'' Maddie said smoothly, snatching Delia's rag from her hand. ''You're going to take a break and tell me what's going on, what's hurting you inside so much that you're working yourself to death.''

"Don't be silly.''

Maddie didn't back down, just kept her caring gaze steadily on Delia. ''I thought you said it went fine with Jacob.''

Delia tried to draw a steady breath and couldn't, nor could she find her calm. She'd been holding back for days now, and it was killing her.

God help her, she'd actually lied to her sisters. She already felt so useless to the ranch. So unnecessary. The shame of failing with her brother had been too much to bear, so instead of telling them the truth—that Jacob had been less than thrilled with the thought of having her as a sister or moving to Idaho—she'd been noncommittal about the entire trip.

And Cade. She'd been noncommittal about him, too.

Maddie was looking at her much as a worried mom would a wayward child, which never failed

to make the usually cool-as-a-cucumber Delia
squirm. No one, certainly not she or Zoe, could
ever hold up against that stare.

Which was funny because Maddie was a small
woman, with the delicate features of a porcelain
doll. But she wasn't nearly as frail as she looked,
not even close. After twenty years together, Delia
thought, she should know.

When they'd been young, Maddie hadn't been
able to speak at first. No one knew what had
caused this trauma, and Delia and Zoe didn't know
to this day, only that she'd come from some hor-
rible situation. But with Delia and Zoe watching
out for her, eventually Maddie had learned to both
speak and smile and even laugh.

Now, years later, Delia was convinced Maddie
was the strongest of all three of them. So strong
that Delia could come clean and sob out all her
woes, but she didn't. She held back with an effort
that had her at the end of her rope. But she had to,
had to be strong to get through this.

Eyes narrowed in deep concern, Maddie came
closer while Delia tried to act tough.

"I'm not going to stand by and let you keep
your hurts to yourself," Maddie told her gently.
"Share."

"Maddie." Delia managed a laugh. "Come on.
We have guests coming tomorrow. We have Zoe's
wedding in three weeks. There's a million things
we need to be doing, not to mention the wedding
dress and two bridesmaid dresses I'm still working

on, all by myself I might add, since the two of you are so pathetic with a needle and thread, and none of it involves spilling my guts—''

Maddie reached out and hugged her tightly.

Delia nearly cracked. While she returned the hug, soothed by Maddie's warm arms, she fought for control. And just barely found it.

''Always so strong,'' Maddie murmured, stroking Delia's hair. ''So independent. It's okay to need someone, Delia. To ask for help. Maybe you'll feel better.''

Help. She had always had a problem asking, mostly because she had learned at an early age that asking meant showing weakness, and showing weakness left her vulnerable.

But this was Maddie, her sister, and one of the two people in the world who loved her unconditionally. She could ask for anything and nothing would be refused.

And wasn't that the problem? The same thought continued to haunt her. How could she put her brother's needs before her sister's? She had no right to ask anyone to give up their dream for hers, no right at all.

''Jacob is okay, right?'' Maddie asked

''Yes, he's…fine.'' *He hates me, but he's fine.*

''And the custody hearing is still on. The judge is still considering you?''

''Yes.'' *Until he looks at my background, combines that with the utter lack of financial security.*

Not to mention Scott, whom I didn't exactly bowl over with my winning personality.

"Well, I, for one, can't wait to get him here and mother him to death." Maddie's smile was soft and full of affection as she pulled back. "He's going to have all the family he ever wanted. It's going to be perfect."

"It is." *She hoped.*

But Maddie wasn't done fretting. "You're not nervous about the guests?"

"No." Delia did smile at that, for this was one thing she was looking forward to. It would certainly keep both her mind and body busy. "But those windows are stressing me out, so—"

"It's Cade, isn't it?"

Delia dropped the bottle of cleaner. Slowly she retrieved it. It took some effort to make sure her voice, when she replied, would be steady, because just hearing his name evoked all sorts of images, mostly being held in those big warm arms and receiving a kiss that days later could still make her knees wobble. "What does he have to do with anything?"

Maddie gave her a long look. "Gee, other than the fact you can't say his name, I don't know. What *does* he have to do with anything?"

"Nothing. I don't know why you'd say it."

"And if someone else says his name, your claws come out."

"I don't know what you're talking about."

Maddie crossed her arms and lifted a brow.

"Not to mention what happens to you when he walks into the room."

"That's ridiculous," Delia scoffed. But what was really ridiculous was that she was a tough sophisticated city girl and hadn't yet managed in all her twenty-six years to lose her virginity. She wasn't sure why exactly, other than that no one had ever come close to making her feel half of what Cade had with one kiss. And yet to him, she was just a case. Probably a nuisance, to boot. He was a roamer, and when he was done here, he'd move on. "Nothing happens when he walks into the room."

Maddie smiled and shook her head, her eyes full of sympathy and humor. "Oh, honey. Something happens all right."

"If you think so, you need glasses."

"You *react*."

"Of course I react. It's a full-blown allergic reaction. The man gives me hives."

"The *man?*" The usually somber Maddie burst out laughing. "Cade. His name is Cade. Come on, I bet it rolls right off your tongue. Try it."

"Yeah. You might like it."

Cade had come into the room—how long ago? Delia wondered wildly—and stood there watching her, his eyes hooded. His arms were crossed over his chest, and on his face, damn him, his laughing mocking face, was the knowledge of what he could—and had—done to her with just one touch.

"Cade." Maddie squeezed Delia's arm gently,

meant to both soothe and warn. "We were just talking about you. I'm making your favorite for dinner—pot roast. You'll stay?"

He smiled at her, his grin crooked, endearing and just a little reckless. "Thanks, it sounds terrific, but I can't. I'm…going."

"You're leaving? I thought you and Ty were busy with the repairs on the back fencing."

"We've finally finished." Languidly, he stretched his back and shoulder muscles, which were clearly outlined beneath his snug T-shirt, and Delia felt a powerful need to rub up against him, a need she assured herself was immature, no matter how hot and deep the ache was.

"You worked so hard."

"Yeah," he agreed. "And given my aches and creaks, I'm getting old. Man, this cowboy stuff is hard work. I gotta hand it to Ty. He's amazing."

He was leaving, was all Delia could think. Going back to the city, probably, and his other cases. Fine. More than fine, actually. Good.

So why did she feel a funny pang in her midsection?

Indigestion.

"I hope Ty thanked you for staying and helping us get ready to open. We needed all the extra hands we could get, but we know you have a life away from here, as well." Maddie squeezed Delia's hands again, another warning. "Don't we, Delia?"

A not-so-subtle hint to add her own thank-you.

Good manners had Delia opening her mouth to do just that, but the words stuck in her throat.

She'd managed to avoid him since they'd returned from Los Angeles. It hadn't been difficult, especially since he had done his own avoiding.

Not exactly complimentary, Delia thought with a frown.

It was one thing for *her* to need her own space, but she didn't think she liked him needing *his* as well. "Going back to Boise?" she asked coolly.

"For a day or so." He lifted one broad shoulder. "I'll be traveling. Have some things to check out."

"The exciting life of a private investigator," Maddie said smiling. "You enjoy this part."

"Very much," he admitted. When he glanced at the door, something inside Delia hardened.

He can't wait to leave.

Never in her life had she felt the urge to cling. She certainly wouldn't start now. But he wanted to leave, couldn't wait to leave, and it was because of her.

The knowledge was deflating. "Well, we don't want to keep you," she said.

Maddie sent Delia a meaningful glare. She wanted Delia to join her in convincing Cade to stay. "Are you sure you can't rearrange things to be here for the grand opening?" Maddie asked him while nudging Delia.

Delia said nothing, didn't add her own request for him to stay. Maddie was on her own there.

Realizing that, her sister sighed. "You've

worked so hard to help us," Maddie said to Cade.
"It'd be a shame if you had to leave just one day
before watching how it all turns out."

Cade looked at Delia, as if waiting for her to
second Maddie's sentiments.

Did he expect her to beg? Ha! He'd have a long
wait if he was. She never begged.

Besides, she wanted him gone.

She did. And if she said it often enough she
might believe it.

"I have things that have to be done," he said,
and Maddie made another sound of disappointment.

"I know you've spent this past year going back
and forth, trying to fit Constance's case into your
heavy workload," Maddie said. "But it seemed
that lately you spent more and more time here,
which we loved. You're a part of our family now,
Cade." She smiled into his surprised face. "And I
got used to you being here. We hate to see you
go."

"I'm sorry." He closed his eyes for a moment.
"I never meant to integrate myself so completely
here or to disrupt—"

"Don't you dare apologize!" Maddie said
fiercely. "You're welcome here, as much as I am
or Ty or Zoe or Delia. You belong here—"

"No," he said quickly. "I don't belong here
or..." He fell silent, and looked out the window.

Or...anywhere? Was that what he'd been about
to say? Delia wondered. Was that why he was al-

ways on the run? He didn't feel as though he belonged anywhere?

For all that Cade McKnight seemed an open book—adventurous, carefree, rugged and tough—she realized there was much about him she didn't know.

Didn't *want* to know, she corrected.

"You need to go," Maddie said softly, coming to terms with his imminent departure.

Cade smiled at her, without the wariness that had been there when he'd looked at Delia. "Yeah."

"I understand," Maddie whispered. "The need to go."

Delia hadn't been able to take her eyes off Cade, so that when he suddenly turned his head to look at her again, she was caught.

Something passed between them, something Delia didn't want to acknowledge, but given the bemusement on his face, he didn't want to acknowledge it, either.

It baffled her, this strange thing that seemed to happen to them whenever they were within close proximity. They had nothing in common, they had completely different goals in life, and yet...there was something that helplessly drew her to him.

But she could control it. She could control all her emotions.

Maddie was still watching the two of them. "Maybe the things you have to go do," she said quietly to Cade, "maybe they could wait for just one more day so you could enjoy all the work you've put into the Triple M?''

When Cade didn't speak, but continued to hold Delia's gaze, Maddie gave a small knowing smile that Cade missed.

Delia did not, and she sent her sister a warning glance.

With a long-practiced skill, Maddie ignored her and moved to the door. ''I think I'll just check on dinner…'' She patted Cade's arm and smiled again when he didn't break eye contact with Delia. ''And leave you two alone to talk this out.''

''Talk what out?'' Delia demanded, but Maddie was gone and Cade was still staring at her, as if he was angry and hurt and confused all at once.

''Why are you always staring at me like that?'' Delia asked.

''I haven't a clue,'' he muttered. ''But I'm outta here.''

''Fine. Great.'' Then words popped right out of her mouth before she could stop them. ''Miss my sister's pot roast and the first guests and everything, I certainly don't care.''

He'd turned toward the door, but went absolutely still at her words, so carelessly tossed out, in spite of the tightness in her chest. ''What are you saying?'' he asked, still facing the door. ''That you don't think I should go?''

She stared at his taut sleek back, her heart racing out of control, and she had no idea why. ''No, of course not. I'm just saying it's really great pot roast, and we all know she made it specially for you, anyway."

Slowly he turned around, his expression carefully masked. "You don't want me to go."

"Don't be ridiculous. I don't care what you do. Go. Stay. It's all the same to me, even if one of the first guests, Tom something or other, is one of your previous clients and is only coming because you recommended him."

"You don't want me to go," he repeated, sounding shocked. "Damn, Delia." In two long-legged strides, he walked toward her and hauled her into his arms, bringing her face close to his tormented one. "What the hell am I going to do with you?"

If she thought her heart had been pounding before at just the sight of him, it was nothing compared to what happened now, when his hands were on her, and his mouth so close to hers she could almost taste him. "You could kiss me again," she whispered, shaken to the core at her wanton suggestion, but not about to take it back.

"I could," he whispered back. "But I'm still leaving."

"Good. Can't wait. Now kiss me, Cade."

"I might." He moved a fraction so that their lips nearly touched. "I also might stay for pot roast."

"And the guests." Was that her voice, all husky and breathless? "Don't forget the guests. You should probably stay long enough to see them, at least.''

''Just to make sure everything goes smoothly. Then I'll go.''

''I'll be counting the minutes until you do. Now kiss me.''

''I suppose I could spare one little goodbye kiss.''

''Big of you.''

''Yes,'' he agreed, shifting slightly so that their hips brushed once, twice, allowing her to feel the hardness of him.

''Do it,'' she demanded, already breathless.

''Come get it.''

Smiling at the rush of feminine power, because nothing made her feel more in control than knowing she was running the show, she pressed her body even closer to his. ''If you insist,'' she murmured, closing her eyes because his were warm and fathomless and much too intense.

She let the kiss take her, until she was dizzy, until she was thrilling to the low rough noise Cade made in his throat when she rubbed against him, until she realized she was getting in far too deep to be able to pull back.

That was unacceptable.

Frightening.

Glorious.

And it had to stop.

She heard Cade's moan of protest when she

pulled away, but all she could do was stare up at him, her lungs straining for air, her mind in a whirl.

His own chest rose and fell harshly, too, his mouth wet from hers. Sanity slowly returned to his dark eyes. "Like I said," he managed, "I haven't a clue about what to do with you."

"Good thing you're leaving soon."

"Very soon."

"And you'll be off and traveling, without a care in the world about what the people close to you think."

"There is no one close to me."

That hurt, she discovered. "My sisters might disagree with that," she said lightly. "But since I know you better than they do, I won't hurt them by telling them."

"Good."

"Good."

"Good," he echoed again, but it was a long moment, during which they just stared at each other, before he turned and walked away.

Chapter 6

The first guests arrived on Thursday. Two couples and a group of four friends. Eight in all, a manageable number, Delia told herself. They would be a success.

They had to be.

Everyone arrived within an hour of one another, giving the three sisters a run for their money.

Maddie's eyes were bright and excited as she rubbed her hands in glee, having caught Delia in the kitchen, where they shared a quick celebratory soda.

"Dinner is going to be spectacular," Maddie whispered joyfully, passing the drink to Delia. "Eight of them, with us it'll be thirteen! It's like a real restaurant!"

Bless Maddie, whose greatest thrill in life was cooking for a captive audience. But she was a terrific cook, a talent that had been long wasted in Los Angeles, where she had never been willing or able to play the political game required to work at any of the "in" restaurants.

But now, for the first time in her life, Maddie was in her true element, and Delia was so happy for her she couldn't resist hugging her.

"I can't believe you're getting this excited," Delia said with a laugh as they twirled around the kitchen. "Have you pictured the dishes? The mess? The demands on your time?"

"Yes, isn't it wonderful?" Maddie's usually serious face split in a wide grin, making her look sixteen, instead of twenty-six.

Delia couldn't hold back another laugh. "We're crazy, you know. All of us."

"Certifiable," Maddie agreed. "And I can't tell you how good that smile looks on your face."

"A full house will do that to me. I'm imagining our happy bank balance."

"Are you?" Maddie's look was long and knowing. "Because I thought maybe Cade had put that look there."

Delia, who'd just taken a sip from the can of soda, choked. Coughing and sputtering, she glared at Maddie.

"Oh, I'm sorry," Maddie said innocently. "I forgot how you react whenever you hear his name."

"Whose name?" Zoe asked as she entered the kitchen, looking tired but happy. "What's up?"

"Nothing," Maddie said. "Other than that Delia seems to have a problem drinking and hearing Cade's name. Or breathing and hearing Cade's name. Or just existing and hearing—"

"You know, until a second ago, you were my favorite sister," Delia said to Maddie.

"Hey, I thought *I* was your favorite sister." Zoe feigned a sulk. "You said so last week when I took over the cleaning of— Wait a minute. *Cade?*" Her eyes narrowed speculatively as she studied Delia with a mixture of disbelief and amusement. "You mean to tell me you have a thing for *Cade?*"

"Say it again and you'll be scrubbing the floor with that mouth, instead of kissing Ty with it."

"You know, you can take the girl out of the city," Zoe said, grinning broadly, "but you sure as hell can't take the city out of the girl. You got a thing for that hot-looking investigator of ours? Really?"

"You're getting married," Delia said through her teeth. "I doubt Ty would appreciate your thinking Cade is hot."

"He's really something, isn't he?" the usually man shy Maddie interjected. "And my, oh my, can he fill out a pair of jeans."

Zoe hooted at this, practically rolling on the floor with mirth. Delia stood still and waited for the moment to pass. "Since I'm the only one with a brain left, I'll go make sure our guests are all comfortable.'' She sent her sisters a look of disgust. "You two stay here and giggle like idiots.''

"You really have a thing for Cade,'' Zoe repeated with marvel. "Oh, just wait until Ty—''

Delia made a grab for Zoe, but experienced with her two hot-tempered sisters, Maddie quickly stepped between them, her eyes still laughing. "Hey. No brawling. I think we should charge extra if you're going to give the clients a show.''

"Fine,'' Delia said, throwing up her hands. "But tell *her* to be quiet. I don't want to hear—''

"Does Cade know you think he's hot?''

"—that name,'' Delia ground out.

"Cade, Cade, Cade,'' Zoe sang, sticking her tongue out at Delia.

"Behave, Zoe,'' Maddie said mildly. "We can't afford to have Delia kill you. We have too much to do.''

"Okay.'' But Zoe was still grinning as she lifted the soda from Delia's hands and took a good long swallow. "But can I tease her later?''

"At your peril,'' Maddie said, and Delia sighed.

"Can't we talk about something else, *anything* else?''

"Oh, all right, fine,'' Zoe said with her own sigh. "Don't admit you have a healthy lust for an absolutely gorgeous man. Deprive yourself—see if I care.'' She turned to Maddie. "Do you need any help with dinner? You're going to have your hands full.''

At the mention of dinner, Maddie's entire face

lit up. "No, of course not. Actually, I almost feel guilty these people are paying us, since I'd do this for free."

"Well, let's be thankful you don't have to." Delia grabbed her soda back from Zoe and finished it off. Just insisting she didn't find Cade attractive had her mouth dry as cotton. "I'm off to make sure everyone's settled." She sent Zoe a withering look. "And if you have so much time on your hands, you can come help me."

Zoe smiled. "Sure, no problem." The minute Delia turned her back to walk down the hall, Zoe whispered the name that sent shivers up her spine. "Cade."

Delia stopped short and drew in a careful breath. "You're cruising."

Zoe laughed uproariously, then slipped an arm around Delia's waist. "You're so easy, Dee."

"You're going to tell Ty, aren't you," she said with dread.

"Oh, yeah."

"And he'll tell... God, this is bad. How much to keep your trap shut?"

"Such sisterly affection." Zoe tsked, then grinned. "Take my chores tonight so I can be alone with Ty."

"You mean—" Delia tried not to grimace "—take care of the animals?"

"Uh-huh."

Both of them knew Delia had never been an animal lover. When they were in Los Angeles, it had never mattered, but out here, where they were now responsible for many animals every day, it'd been quite an adjustment.

Now, thanks to her own stupidity, she'd have to feed and water all of them, on her own, and she knew damn well there were huge spiders lurking everywhere in that barn. While she would have liked to grimace, it would show her fear, which Delia hated to do. "I'm truly going to kick your butt, Zoe," she said, instead.

"Tomorrow. I'm busy tonight." Her sister lifted her brows suggestively.

"And you'll keep your mouth shut, right?"

"Right." She grinned at Delia. "I love you, you know."

"I'm still going to kick your butt."

Zoe sighed fondly. "You love me, too."

They survived their first day. It had taken them a while to get into their stride, but they'd done it. To settle herself down after supper, Delia worked on Zoe's wedding dress for a time, enjoying the physical work and mental freedom as she stitched the fine lace and ivory silk dress from the pattern she'd created.

Eventually she had to set it aside because she had to do Zoe's chores, which made her shudder in distaste. She entered the barn, prepared to hate the duty, even though secretly she was glad for the opportunity to help Zoe, who worked far too hard.

Delia worked hard, too, but her work was different, and while she wanted—needed—to do her fair share, she'd always felt her contribution to the ranch was negligible.

Guilt gnawed at her, it always did, because she'd have given anything to be needed here.

Thinking about being needed led her to worrying about Jacob and custody, which of course led her to think about the Triple M and its hopeful success, which led her to thinking about her future.

And that, for some ridiculous reason, brought her full circle to Cade. It was ridiculous because he had no intention of ever being part of anyone's future, much less hers.

Delia sighed and turned on the lights. Just as she imagined, a huge black spider scurried from its resting place on the lightswitch and she nearly fell in her haste to back up. Shuddering, she wiped her fingers on her jeans, even though she hadn't touched it. "Yuck," she muttered. "There aren't spiders that gross in the city, that's for certain."

Maybe not, but at least here, she had a shot of owning something for the first time in her life.

It was thrilling. Yes, each of the three sisters had wanted to be heir. It would give the deserted foster children they'd once been a heritage. A name. But it had nothing to do with greed, for no matter which of them inherited, the three of them would share equally.

Equally.

However, that wouldn't get her Jacob.

Delia hated her lack of security; she always had.

It had nothing to do with money. No, that would make her little better than her own mother had been.

It definitely had nothing to do with money.

And everything to do with worth. Self-worth. Confidence. Two things she could pretend to have fairly well but had never sincerely experienced.

And speaking of confidence… Nervously she moved from the barn door and stared at the double row of horses. "At least Zoe and Ty put you all up for the night," she said, and several curious heads peered over the stall doors.

The one closest to her nickered softly, and Delia nearly parted company with her skin. "Okay, I can do this," she whispered. "Hey…you guys hungry?"

Another nicker, this one not so soft and from the big guy at the end of the line. "No problem," she said, mostly to herself. She even added a smile as she cautiously moved to where the supplies were. "Just between you and me," she said conversationally, "Zoe is dead meat."

She had all the horses watching her now, some more vocal than others. "You guys are a great audience." Gaining a bit more confidence, she looked into Betsy's eyes, the mare she'd ridden. "Give me a clue here, could you? Zoe's told me a million times how much feed to give you, not that I listened."

Betsy tossed her head.

"Hey, I'm trying." She pulled on a pair of

leather gloves, because having to do chores didn't
mean she had to ruin her manicure. Then, because
it was there, she added a full-chested leather apron.
"No sense in ruining perfectly perfect clothes,"
she told Betsy. "Handmade, you know." She
pointed to her black linen trousers and soft angora
sweater. With a resigned sigh, she hefted a pitchfork. "Wow, this sucker's heavy. I'm going to
have to rethink kicking Zoe's butt if she can do
this twice a day."

The big horse at the end of the row snorted, and
Delia looked at him. "You got something to say?"

He just stared at her, and she could have sworn
his eyes were laughing at her. Laughing.

Like Cade's.

"Men," she muttered. "You're all alike. You
all think you can bat those long lashes and we'll
melt at your feet." If she realized she was talking
about Cade's eyes, it didn't matter, no one could
hear her. "And please, don't get me started on the
smile thing. I swear, you all think a simple smile
will leave us boneless and panting."

"We can hope." It was Cade's voice that had
her boneless now. "And there's a frown that will
scare away guests."

Jerked out of her thoughts, her heart ricocheting
madly off her ribs, Delia slowly turned around and
managed to look cool. "You have a thing for
sneaking up on me. Stop it." She ran a hand down
the apron, ostensibly to smooth it, but she was really pressing her hand to her racing heart to keep

it from galloping away. "And for the record, I never frown."

"Of course not. It'd give you wrinkles."

"Bite your tongue." She lifted her chin, and though she felt oddly weak when she wanted to be strong, she leaned on the pitchfork and studied him.

It wasn't a hardship. He was definitely a sight that would have made a weaker female than she sigh with longing. His long lean legs were lovingly encased in soft worn denim. He wore a flannel shirt, unbuttoned over a T-shirt. Plain clothes, but they somehow took on a life of their own when stretched over his big tough body. He looked rugged...and sinful.

And the way her body tightened, almost as if in anticipation, really annoyed her.

Since when had she lost control of herself when it came to this man? "What do you want?"

Cade pondered the question as if she seriously wanted an answer. *What did he want?* Lots of things, most of which would probably send her screaming from the barn if she knew.

He wanted her to drop her guard around him.

He wanted to haul her close.

He wanted to be far away so that he could stop thinking about her night and day.

But mostly he wanted...her. He wanted Delia Scanlon, the woman.

Telling her that would only give her the ammunition she needed to further retreat and hide from him. "Do you always talk to the animals?" he asked. "Or is it a full moon?"

"Were you eavesdropping on me?"

"No."

Relief flickered across her features until he spoke again. "Does my smile leave you as boneless as my horse's?"

Now those eyes that so fascinated him flashed with anger and a good amount of embarrassment. "You *were* eavesdropping on me. How dare you?"

He'd dare anything for her. He was certain she had no idea how sexy she looked with the gloves too large for her hands, the leather apron dwarfing her lovely body, her eyes filled with confusion. She had no idea what she was doing out here, but heaven forbid she admit that, or admit she needed his help. She was adorable. Irresistible. Dammit.

"I came right through the open door, Delia." He gestured and she tossed an angry glare over her shoulder to see for herself.

Indeed the door was wide open, revealing the dark night and starlit sky. It was a sight that never failed to stab directly into his heart, because when he was here, on this mountain out in the middle of nowhere, he felt safe. He felt as though he were home. He felt warm and fuzzy, even happy.

Not that he wanted to feel safe. Or at home. He sure as hell didn't want to feel warm and fuzzy. These were emotions and feelings he didn't allow himself.

"Just so you don't stroke that ego any more than necessary," Delia said. "It wasn't *your* smile I was talking about."

Good. That was good. It would help during those dark hours of the night when he couldn't sleep, couldn't do anything but think about how she felt in his arms. "I'll remember that," he said, moving farther into the barn.

Her eyes widened slightly at his proximity, the only sign she gave that he did indeed affect her every bit as much as she affected him.

And as much as he might like to explore the physical aspect of that, he couldn't. Delia was different. He couldn't imagine her taking any part of a relationship lightly, especially sex. No, she wouldn't give herself without love, and since he didn't do love, not anymore, they were destined to do this strange emotional two-step around each other.

Maybe it was to be his own personal penance for what he'd lost, but he would have thought just being alive when his wife and son were not was enough. Whatever it was, it was *his* hell, not hers, and he needed to remember that.

As if that would help keep his hands and mind off her.

"And I can resist you," she said coolly as she took a step back, dropping the pitchfork she obviously had no idea how to use. "Just in case you were wondering."

He came closer because he had to. "Because we aren't suited."

"Exactly," she said, taking another step back.

Which he, of course, ignored as he came closer still. She smelled like heaven—sweet yet unbearably sexy. "And again, why is it we're not suited?"

"Because you're…you're, you know. Wild. Rowdy. *Uncontrollable.*"

She said the last as if it was an unforgivable sin.

"Ah, that's it," he said. "Misbehaving, rough, ungroomed Cade McKnight. Dangerous. Edgy. Unsuitable. Right?"

A flicker of regret crossed her face. "I can't be telling you anything you don't know." She was right. He did know.

So why was he pushing her?

"Why are you here?" she asked again, watching him with that slight vulnerability through her cool veneer, one that never failed to tug directly on the heart he wanted to be dead.

"I have something on the inheritance case," he said, cursing himself for forgetting, even for one moment, how important this would be to her.

"What?" She took a step toward him and grabbed his shirt in her fists. "Tell me! What did you find?"

Her eyes were wide. Eager. And his heart ached again. "I finally got my hands on a copy of your mother's death certificate. There's an address listed."

"Okay." She processed this, then, still holding on to him, gave him a little shake. "What else?"

"I was able to locate the owner of the property, who told me an old friend of your mother's still lives in the building. Dottie Owens. I'm going to go see her—maybe she'll know something about your father."

"In Los Angeles?"

Her fierce determination made him wary. So did the death grip she had on his shirt, which also involved a few chest hairs. "Yes."

"I'm going with you."

"Delia—"

"Don't even try to stop me."

He remembered when he'd accompanied her on her trip to see Jacob, remembered how, in spite of her anger, she'd appreciated the company, whether she admitted it or not.

Somehow, in reverse, he didn't think he would appreciate her company, not when everything about her—her hope, her warmth, her independence, her strength—was packaged into one beautiful willowy desirable woman who drew him as no other had in far too long. "No," he said hoarsely.

"Yes."

So much for getting away from her.

Chapter 7

The outdoors had never attracted Delia before. That it did now was a source of wonder. Normally the land was rich with vibrant colors, but now, facing the onset of cold weather, a sort of hush had fallen over the land.

Delia pulled on a heavy coat and gloves, drawn by something she didn't understand, and made her way to the bluff overlooking the river.

There she stood, staring down at the awesome sight of the rushing water, thinking how this land didn't seem so alien now. That maybe it had started to worm its way into her resistant heart.

You're coming back...to see me?

The words echoed in her head from the phone conversation she'd just had with Jacob. He'd been taken off guard and, being so young, had been unable to hold back his first reaction, which had been hopeful joy.

Then he'd caught himself and had reined in his emotions. "Didn't think you'd come back home," he'd stated.

"I'm coming back," Delia had said, her voice a little thick with emotion, "over and over again. But my home...is here in Idaho." And for the first time she really believed that, and it felt good. Into his bleak silence, she'd said, "Maybe you'll want to come here someday."

More silence.

"We have animals here," she said desperately.

"Like horses?"

"Lots. You could ride one if you like." It was pure bribery, but she'd use whatever it took.

"That'd be fine," he'd said casually, but he hadn't fooled Delia. It wasn't indifference he felt, only fear, which broke her heart. He was testing her, making sure she was going to stick around.

Which she was, through thick and thin. He'd never be disappointed by family again.

She heard a horse approaching from behind, and thinking Zoe had come seeking her out, she turned with a smile meant to assure her sister she was all right.

And met Cade's gaze, instead.

He was still fifty feet back. Would he actually acknowledge her, she wondered, or ignore her as he'd done his best to do these past few days?

Granted, they'd all been busy with their guests, but it was more than that. For whatever reason, ever since he'd told her of his lead, Cade had backed off.

She told herself that was just fine with her, but she still tensed at the mere sight of him.

A gust of icy wind blew, loosening her hair so that it whipped her face. Below them the roar of the water blended with the sound of the wind and the rustling trees, producing a symphony only Mother Nature could create.

Delia shivered, but it was more from a heightened sense of awareness than the actual cold. Still, she was grateful for the sun beaming down on them, weak as it was.

After a long moment, Cade nudged his horse closer, then closer still, and her breath caught in a vexing sort of anticipation, because no matter how she tried to put it out of her mind that only this man could make her ache and burn, her body would never let her forget.

Only the knowledge that he could obviously turn the heat on and off, that he could plan on leaving and not worry about coming back, kept her cool.

Cade swung down from the saddle, murmured something to his horse and came closer still.

"You look at home," he said.

She shrugged, having finally found her mental distance. "Tell that to Zoe, who thinks I'll never give up my city ways." Delia didn't have to admit she still missed the city—the malls, the grumpy crowds, the restaurants. The culture. She missed it all, but much in the way one missed school once it was out. It was with a sort of fondness, not any real ache.

In spite of herself, this place was becoming home. Tilting her head back, she studied the sky. No smog. No planes. Just glorious brilliant blue sky.

"We need to leave in an hour," he said.

"I'm packed and ready to go." They'd go together, investigate the address he had. Then she'd see Jacob and come back to the ranch, to her home.

As for Cade, he'd be off. She had no idea when she'd see him again, but she considered that a good thing.

Their guests had gone, and when they'd left, they'd been full, content, happy and thrilled with their experience.

Delia was happy, too, and knowing she had until Thursday before the next group of guests arrived helped ease her guilt at leaving her sisters for a few days.

They didn't need her, she reminded herself. They'd function fine without her. Fact was, neither Zoe nor Maddie resented her trip in the least, but she felt a moment of shame that she'd expected them, too.

They loved her, and even after twenty years, the knowledge still thrilled her. What *didn't* thrill her was the thought of yet another trip with the tall enigmatic man in front of her. But she couldn't let

him go without her. She had too much at stake,
not to mention years of curiosity and buried hurt.

"I know you're packed," he said quietly. "But
are you really ready?"

"Does it matter?"

He stared at her a moment before turning his
too-intense gaze to the river. The wind continued
to tug at them, at her clothes and his, at the long-
sleeved shirt he wore, molding it to his chest and
back.

"It matters," he said grimly. "*You* matter."

"But you don't want me to matter."

"No more than you want me to matter to you."

Well, he had her there.

"I know why *I* resist this…this *thing* between
us," she said. "But why do you? What's haunting
you, Cade?"

His jaw hardened. He slipped his hands into his
pockets. "Nothing I'm willing to talk about."

Fair enough, she supposed. And not for the first
time, she realized it was almost comforting to
know it would never go further than this, that sex-
ual attraction was all they had. Lust could be ignored.

Their arms brushed lightly.

And she had to tell herself again that all they
had was that lust, nothing more. But the truth was,
his touch soothed her. His strength fed hers.

How could this happen when her own strength
had always been enough?

"I don't know what we'll find," he said. "But it might be rough on you—"

"I'm going."

"Okay, but—"

"No. No buts." She sighed, speaking her thoughts out loud, shocking herself with the weakness she couldn't control. "Why do you think my mother didn't want me?"

He looked at her with a mixture of surprise and a compassion far too close to pity. She turned away and added quickly, "I was a pretty good kid, I was…just wondering, and…"

"Delia—"

"No, I'm sorry." She let out a laugh that sounded pathetically close to a sob. "It's nothing."

"God, Delia," he murmured, turning her to face him. "How long have you been thinking about this?"

"Forever," she whispered. Then, "Look, forget it," she said. "Please, just forget I said anything. I'll meet you inside when you're ready—"

He stopped her with a finger to her lips. "Your mother wasn't good enough for you, not even close. No mother should be able to walk away from her child."

Delia was a tall woman, but he was much taller, so that her gaze fell directly on his wide, generous mouth, his square jaw, which at this moment was hard with anger.

Anger for her, she realized with some surprise and an odd little shiver.

"I don't know if your father knew who you were," he said, his tone intense. "Or even if he was Constance's son Ethan Freeman, but I swear we'll find out. For once and for all, you'll know your past. You won't have to wonder anymore."

It would be a double-edged sword, the knowing. Her past would no longer be a mystery. And if her father turned out to be the no-good drifter, liar, user, Ethan Freeman, then she would have gotten what she needed—the inheritance necessary to get Jacob.

She'd know her own gene pool—and the fact she'd come from two complete losers.

"Are you sure?" he whispered. "You don't have to do this."

"Yes, I do."

In Cade's opinion, Los Angeles was a chameleon. Whatever one desired, it could be had, whether it was fun or serious, whether you were rich or poor.

A place to succeed or merely survive.

The heat was oppressive, unusually heavy and sticky. They drove to a seedy subdivision, long past its prime.

Delia looked shocked when he pulled up to a run-down apartment complex with neglected palm trees drooping in front of a wrought-iron gate half-fallen down.

"My mother lived here? Are you sure?"

"It's her last known address, according to her

D.M.V. records.'' He hated knowing he was destroying whatever positive memories Delia had managed to retain, but to learn the truth about her father, it had to be done. ''It's been over twenty years. Things change.''

''Yes.''

She looked out of place as she got out of the car: tall, willowy, coolly beautiful. She wore a fitted sundress the color of a ripe peach, which looked elegant and sophisticated. Hard to imagine her fitting into this life, but Cade knew that was exactly what would have happened if her mother hadn't taken her to the foster home.

She would have grown up here.

He wondered if Delia, staring at the building with an unreadable expression on her face, was thinking the same thing.

Then he remembered he wasn't supposed to care what the hell she thought. ''Come on,'' he said gruffly, and led the way. ''Let's go get your answers.''

The main door was unlocked. They entered and moved down the hall. When they knocked on the door, a woman answered. Her clothes were rumpled, her hair disheveled. On her face was at least day-old makeup. That hard prematurely aged face twisted into a frown at the sight of them. ''What do you want?'' she asked.

''Dottie?'' Cade gave her a smile.

''Yeah.'' She looked him over. ''So?''

"Cade McKnight. I spoke with you on the phone regarding Evelyn Scanlon."

Dottie glanced at Delia, then did a comical double take. "Lord, girl, you look just like your momma."

Delia didn't so much as blink, not the cool unflappable Delia, but Cade knew that bit of news had rocked her to the core.

"It's like going back in time," Dottie said, awed, shaking her head. "Just like her."

"Can we ask you some questions?"

Dottie's gaze slid back to Cade. "You a cop?"

"No, ma'am, a private investigator. Like I told you, we're trying to locate Ms. Scanlon's father."

Dottie snorted indelicately. "Good luck."

Delia broke her silence. "You knew him?"

"No one knew him."

"Are you certain?"

"As certain as I am that I'm standing here wasting my time. He was a selfish pig. What do you want to know about him for?"

"Just for…me," Delia said. "Thank you for your help." Her voice was steady. Totally in control.

Cade knew a lot about hiding feelings. When Lisa and Tommy had first died, he'd hidden everything, not just from others, but from himself. All sadness, all grief, all fury at the injustice of it, everything. It had nearly destroyed him. Before he'd realized it, he was dead inside. A bad thing for an attorney, and a high-powered one at that.

He'd walked away from his cases, had turned away from his family and friends. He'd not been satisfied until nothing of his former life remained. Now, years later, he didn't bother to hide his feelings anymore. He didn't have to. He hardly had any.

Or he hadn't, until Delia. Beautiful stoic hurting Delia. So cool, so calm. He wondered how long she could sustain it. She'd been doing this for what…over twenty years now? When did she allow herself to break? To need someone?

Dammit, she was just a case to him. Nothing more.

As soon as he was done here, he was leaving, going back to his unfeeling self. He'd start with New York. He needed the big city, needed to get lost in it. He had another case with a lead that led there, so he would enjoy himself and take his time.

After that, he thought Florida might suit him.

He'd have to check on Constance's inheritance and the ranch, but he could do that by phone, as well as any follow-up required.

As soon as this business was finished. "On the phone," he said, "you hinted you might be able to give us some insight as to Delia's father's whereabouts."

"Did I?" Dottie straightened away from the door and eyed their clothing with disdain. "Seems anyone that dresses as fancy as you two should be able to pay for whatever they want."

Cade wasn't wearing anything other than casual khaki pants and a tucked-in polo shirt, but he was clean and neat and, he supposed, far cleaner and neater than Dottie. Combined with Delia's unmistakable presence, which she would have exuded even in a potato sack, he could see why Dottie felt they'd come from a different world.

With an outward smile and an inward sigh, he pulled out his wallet.

Dottie brightened considerably. "That's right," she said, rubbing her palms on her thighs, nearly drooling in the process. "Make me an offer."

"Cade…"

Cade shook his head at Delia and offered Dottie several bills. She stuffed them down her top and smiled warmly. "What exactly was it you wanted to know?"

"For starters, his name," Cade said. "Delia's birth certificate doesn't list him."

"A name doesn't mean anything."

"It would be a start," Cade said patiently.

"I'm not certain I can remember." Dottie smiled, crossed her arms.

Cade stared at her, then took out his wallet once more and handed her another bill.

"Cade…"

Again he shook his head, holding eye contact with Dottie. Unfortunately he knew the type. Only money, and maybe intimidation, could reach her.

"I think it was…Eddie," she said. "Eddie something. Eddie Kitze?"

She spelled it for him, and Cade wrote it down. "He said he was a cop. With which department?"

"Never said."

"Never?"

"Just said so, didn't I?"

"Tell us about him."

Dottie rolled her eyes, popped her gum. "Delia's mother was only staying here with friends on and off—she didn't live here. She had a rich daddy, but he was real strict, always kept her on a short leash that she was forever tugging at, you know?"

"You mean she'd run away?"

"No, she wasn't stupid. She snuck out. She enjoyed slumming around."

"Slumming?" Delia repeated, her voice still perfectly even, so much so that Cade narrowed his eyes at her.

It wasn't natural to hide all that emotion.

"Slumming," Dottie said again. "She liked fast cars and faster men. This Eddie, he'd led her to believe he was a real somebody, but when she got herself knocked up, he took off. Never saw him again."

From inside the apartment, a rough male voice called out Dottie's name.

She rolled her eyes again. "Gotta go."

"Wait." Delia took a step toward Dottie, one hand raised in entreaty.

Dottie stepped back. "That's it, sweetcakes. I've gotta run."

The door shut in their faces.

Delia stared at it, not moving, her hand still raised.

Cade's heart twisted. "Delia—"

"Don't," she whispered, dropping her hand and turning away. "Just...don't."

She walked back through the building, down the steps and into the car, all in a terrible heavy silence. When Cade climbed in next to her, she was looking out the window, studying the building.

"Just drop me off at the car-rental place," she said. "I'll need my own car to go see Jacob. And you'll need to get going, I imagine."

Yes, he needed to get going. Wanted to get going. Couldn't *wait* to get going.

"Delia—"

"Just drive, Cade."

"We have a name now," he said, not starting the car, needing to make her feel better somehow. He didn't understand it, this urge he had to make her happy. "With it I can start an effective trace."

She lifted a shoulder as if she didn't care what he did. "The name probably wasn't real."

"I'll find something," he promised rashly, anything to break through that wall she'd erected. "You never know, it could lead us right to—"

"Don't say it," she said in a surprisingly harsh voice. "We've got exactly what we had before you spent two hundred dollars on a junkie. Nothing."

"I don't get it. You were so hot to resolve this thing. How the hell can you just give up?" he demanded, satisfied when hot sparks shot from her eyes.

"I'm not giving up. I never give up."

"Then where's your excitement? Your hope?" Ruthlessly he pushed her, needing to punish her for being so...so everything he wanted and wouldn't let himself have. "We've just been given a good solid lead that could open the door on your past, a past you've wondered about your entire life, and you're sitting there as if it doesn't matter."

"You have no idea what you're talking about."

"Then tell me."

He was practically shouting at her, but dammit, he had this bone-deep need to break through, just for once, and see the real Delia.

"Why should I? You've made it clear we don't mean anything to each other."

"I've made it clear..." He gaped at her, because it was true and he had no idea what to say. He'd never purposely hurt anyone, especially Delia, but she was right in a way. He didn't *want* them to mean anything to each other. And yet it was too late. He let out a long breath. "I'm sorry. It's just that this sizzling attraction between us... Damn, Delia, when I kiss you, I could..."

"You could...?"

He could see his future in her warm loving arms. Told himself he could live happily ever after just being with her, watching her smile, hearing her talk. "Nothing," he said shortly. "Forget it."

"All right, I will."

Great. Jamming the car in drive, he took them out of the seedy neighborhood, letting the road occupy his mind. When they arrived back at the car-rental place, they got out in silence.

"Thank you," she said stiffly, looking cool and elegant. Untouchable. Her hair was in perfect order, the glorious strands shining like spun gold.

The heat was getting to him, he decided. But there was no denying she was a Southern Californian at heart. He wondered if she knew how at home she looked here.

"Let me know what you find out about Eddie Kitze," she said, as if they were discussing dinner plans, instead of her life.

"I wasn't too sure it mattered," he said, openly baiting her, but he was confused, hot and turned on, a combination guaranteed to mess with his head. "What with your overwhelming excitement and all."

The sarcasm had her jaw tightening. "You want a reaction from me?"

"Please."

"Are you certain that won't be getting too personal?"

"Just tell me."

"I think you're moody and impossible to get along with."

He couldn't help it. He laughed. "*I'm* moody?"

She didn't crack a smile. "I think it's ridiculous to even think about anything between us when neither of us seems to be able to act maturely about the whole thing.''

"Assuming I agree with you," he said tightly, not about to admit otherwise, "and we stick to the case, what did you think of what Dottie told us?"

"I think Eddie Kitze lied through his teeth. You won't find him on any police department, because he wasn't a cop. Eddie Kitze...Ethan Constance. They could have been one and the same." She surprised him by showing emotion. Her voice revved up as she spoke. Her color heightened. "So assuming Dottie wasn't lying and assuming Eddie was and that he was really Ethan, I could get Jacob. Also assuming, of course, that he wants to come."

"Delia—"

"No, please, don't give me empty assurances, because really, the truth is, he resents the hell out of me right now."

Suddenly she sighed and hung her head, showing a weariness he'd only guessed at. She rubbed her temples. "God," she whispered, "all the ifs. It's killing me." Then she lifted her head and gazed at him with haunted eyes, making him more than a little sorry he'd pushed her for a reaction.

"And then there's you," she whispered. "Driving me crazy. Coming. Going. Coming..." She sighed. "I really want you to just go somewhere and stay there."

"I am going," he said, but because he was still an idiot, he pulled her close, instead.

Her arms snaked around his neck. "I'm mad at you," she whispered, pressing close.

"I know." His hands slid down her slim back, over her hips, then up again. He couldn't get enough of her.

Together they stood there, clinging, both in heaven and misery, and more confused than ever.

Chapter 8

Scott was waiting for her outside Edna's house. Delia parked and took her time getting out of the car. She was feeling a bit raw and shaky.

Standing by her car, she tilted her face toward the hot sun and took a deep calming breath.

For the first time she could allow herself to believe her hopes had some foundation. Her father *could* have been Constance Freeman's son.

She could be the heir.

If so, it would give her everything she'd ever wanted in one shot. Self-worth, pride.

And Jacob.

With all that to dwell on, it seemed odd that her thoughts were miles away, on another problem entirely. A rugged tough sexy investigator.

There'd been quite a few firsts today. The hope about being the heir and now... For the first time in her life, she actually *wanted* a man, so much so that she trembled at the mere thought. Not a fearful tremble, either, but a sort of secret thrilling anticipating one that made it hard to function.

And Scott was watching her, gauging her worth for Jacob, and there she stood, lost in fantasyland, dreaming about warm arms and drugging kisses.

Smoothing down her dress, she took another deep breath, this one to steady her pulse, and moved up the walk.

"Good afternoon," Scott said formally. Behind his polite smile, his eyes were quiet and assessing, but Delia knew he would find nothing faulty with her appearance, she'd made sure of it.

She was dressed neatly and conservatively in a sundress she'd made herself. No one would have guessed, and it wasn't pride that told her so, but in fact, if there was one thing she could do well, it was look good. She gave a businesslike smile. "I didn't expect to see you today."

"You called for a visit with Jacob."

"And my visits are always going to be supervised?"

"It's a good idea, Delia, for his sake."

"Do you think I'd hurt him?"

Annoyance flickered across Scott's face. "It has nothing to do with you. It's the way this works."

"The system is overworked and underfunded.

Jacob's lucky to have such a dedicated social worker,'' Delia commented.

"Yes, well, I am dedicated to Jacob. He's a special kid.''

Delia felt a pang of guilt for her pettiness, because there was nothing but honesty in Scott's eyes, nothing but true concern for her brother. She was the last one in the world to resent that. "The custody hearing is only a few weeks away,'' she said evenly. "What do you think my chances are?''

"The judge will make that decision.''

"Yes, but that decision will be based, in part, on your recommendation and reports.''

"Are you asking me where I think Jacob should be?''

"Yes,'' she said with equal bluntness. Pride had no place here. "That's what I'm asking.''

"Edna has more money than Jacob's inheritance. She can and will manage it well.''

"And I can't?''

"I didn't say that.''

"I can hire someone to handle his money. I would never touch it.''

He didn't soften. "Then there's the fact that you live so far away. You'd be taking him from everyone and everything he's ever known.''

"Life has already done that to him,'' Delia argued quietly. "I'd be taking him to a place where he could grow up with love and affection and wide-open spaces. He'd have everything he ever needed.''

Scott nodded in reluctant agreement. ''That's true. And to be honest, Edna's age works against her, as does the fact that she didn't go looking for him. He was pretty much dumped on her. Plus, you're his half sister.''

''So you're saying I have a chance?''

''I have nothing to do with the final decision.''

''Scott.''

''I won't give you false hope, Delia. You have several things against you, mostly your lack of financial solvency.'' Seeing the stricken look on her face, he sighed. ''Look, you asked. Now let's go. Jacob's out back playing basketball.''

Burning with the need to prove herself, Delia followed Scott around to the backyard.

Jacob saw Scott and grinned. Then he saw Delia and his smile faded.

''Hi, Jacob,'' she said, forcing herself to stay back when what she really wanted to do was hug him close. ''It's great to see you again.''

''Yeah.'' He blew a big bubble from the wad of gum and shrugged. He'd turned slightly away from her, but glanced back at her as if he wasn't quite sure whether or not she was real.

Her heart nearly burst, and ignoring the distance he clearly still needed, she moved closer, stopping directly in front of him and hunkering down to his level.

''I missed you,'' she said simply.

He stared at his sneakers. "You came."

A knot lodged in her throat because she could see that her presence was a surprise to him, even though she'd called. "I'll always do what I say. I promise."

His only response was a shrug. Delia imagined he'd had lots of promises broken in his past, but that, too, was going to change. "Want to play?" she asked, gesturing to the ball he carried.

"You any good?"

She laughed at his skepticism and kicked off her heeled sandals. "I grew up with a sister who was the best, and I couldn't stand to lose. So, yeah, I'm pretty good."

"Your foster sister," he said.

She watched him carefully. Was he jealous? Excited? Indifferent? "Yes, one of my foster sisters. Zoe and Maddie were all I had for a very long time. Until you."

"Foster sisters aren't really related."

"Not by blood maybe, but in our hearts we are."

"We're blood-related, but it doesn't feel like it."

"It does for me," she said softly. "From the first moment I learned about you, I felt you in my heart. I'm hoping you grow to feel the same."

He thought about that, then with the ease of the very young, he changed the uncomfortable subject. "Which of them can play? Zoe or Maddie?"

"Zoe. I have pictures that I brought with me. Of

my life in Idaho and the people there. Zoe, Maddie. Zoe's fiancé, Ty. Want to see them?''

He lifted his shoulder again. ''You going to play or what?''

''Oh, we're going to play. We'll look at the pictures after I beat you,'' she teased.

''I'm not going to lose to you.'' Then he looked directly at her, for the first time since she'd gotten there, and his eyes filled with a fierce pride she knew well.

It was like looking into a mirror, and it took a moment before she could answer. ''Well, let's see if you're as good as you say.''

''I am.''

Delia silently thanked all those torturous days she'd played with Zoe when they'd been young, for in truth, Jacob was good. Better than good. In less than fifteen minutes, she was laughing and admitting defeat.

Cocky, he held the ball and watched as she bent over, trying to catch her breath. She expected him to make fun of her, but all he said was, ''You're in pretty good shape.''

Lifting her head, she stared at him in surprise.

''For an old chick in a silly dress,'' he added.

Scott, who'd been watching from the sidelines, laughed. ''Not the way to a woman's heart, sport. Never mention their age. And most definitely not their appearance.''

Jacob's smile faded. ''Sorry,'' he mumbled, and turned away.

Delia could have cheerfully strangled Scott, who had, admittedly, been only teasing. But clearly Jacob thought he'd insulted her and now was either wary or embarrassed.

"Ready to see those pictures?" she said, trying to get the good mood back.

But Jacob merely shrugged, his back to her, and for the rest of the day, he was unreachable.

The next group of guests arrived at the Triple M. It was easier this time, especially since the three sisters and Ty knew what to expect.

Maddie outdid herself in the kitchen. Ty and Zoe were a complete success with a mock roundup.

And Delia, without the distraction of the unbearably sexy Cade, found herself enjoying running the house. The hard work kept both her hands and her mind busy, which was exactly what she needed.

The wedding plans helped, too, especially since when she was sewing, she felt validated. One thing she could most definitely do, and do well, was sew.

But through it all, she counted down the calendar toward the custody hearing, which would occur only days after Zoe's wedding, wondering as she did how Cade was coming along on the lead about her father.

Several times each of her sisters had pressed her about Cade, always with that hopeful speculative gleam in their eyes.

They wanted to know what was going on.

Nothing, Delia always claimed, but no one seemed to believe her.

Cade was interested, no doubt. She knew that from his hot looks and even hotter kisses. But he wasn't interested enough to want more, wasn't interested in sharing himself.

She was better off without him.

Or so she told herself in the deep of the night when she awoke with that strange haunting need to be held against a man's warm hard body. And not just any man, but one with fathomless dark eyes and the ability to see past her facade.

On Saturday, as she was racing down the back hallway, a pile of fresh towels in her arms, she heard the office phone ring. She thought about not getting it, but it could be someone wanting reservations, which in turn equaled cash.

Money was still in short supply. But they were booked for nearly every available weekend, so things were looking up. Breathless, Delia slipped into the office, juggled the load of towels in her arms and pushed the speaker button, just as Maddie and Zoe came running from opposite directions, each looking every bit as harried as she did.

"Hello, Triple M," Delia said, just as Maddie and Zoe came to a skidding halt, nearly colliding in the hallway. Delia waved and they waved right back before turning back to whatever they'd dropped to answer the phone.

The voice of Edna on the speaker stopped them all short.

"Jacob," Delia said quickly. "Is he all right?"

"Oh, of course he is. Brought in a lizard not too long ago," the older woman said dryly. "Lovely. Anyway, we got to talking. Jacob mentioned he might like to visit Idaho."

"And bring his lizard?" Zoe asked teasingly.

Delia managed the introductions, hardly hearing a word that was said. She'd nearly dropped her load of towels in shock at the casually worded request from Edna.

With a sweet knowing smile, Maddie came forward and gently took the load from Delia's arms. Zoe, not so gently, pushed the shaky Delia into the nearest chair, for which she was thankful since her knees were shaking.

Jacob wanted to come to Idaho.

Delia drew in a deep breath to remain calm. Or at least sound calm. "Anytime," she said to Edna. "Come anytime at all. Actually, now works for me."

Edna laughed. "Oh, wonderful. Do you have room for us next weekend?"

They had their hands full, most definitely, but they weren't filled to capacity. Still, they were new at this, and her sisters might not appreciate the extra burden on such short notice.

Delia looked over at them. Both were nodding their heads, smiling their encouragement.

Their support caused such a rush of affection she could hardly put her words together. "We have room," she said, her voice husky with emotion. "We'll always have room."

"Then we'll be there," Edna said.

And Delia had to put her head down between her knees.

"They're here," Delia whispered, suddenly terrified, as she looked out the front window of the big house.

Zoe peeked past her. "Hmm. Pretty skinny, isn't he?"

Maddie squeezed between them to stare, as well. "He's just a baby! Oh, look at him, how sweet, pretending he's not dying of curiosity. You know, I can have him fattened up in no time."

Delia gripped the curtains, watching her brother hop out of Ty's truck. Edna followed, with Ty's help. "I hope she isn't insulted that we sent Ty for her."

"She knows we have a full house," Maddie assured her. "She understands. Oh, look at Jacob's face. He's just the cutest thing."

His eyes lit with excitement, Jacob turned toward the barn, then the horses in the corral.

"City boy," Zoe said with a fond sigh. "We'll have to fix that."

Delia just soaked up the very welcome sight of him. Whether he admitted it to her or not, he'd told Edna he wanted to come.

She'd hold that knowledge close to her heart.

"You're shaking," Zoe told her.

"I am not."

Maddie touched her arm. "Dee, it's okay to be nervous."

"I'm not."

Zoe snorted. "You're terrified. Of a little boy."

Delia glared at her, but Maddie, ever the peacemaker, stood between them. "She's teasing you, Delia, and if you weren't so preoccupied, you'd know that and ignore her. Honey, look, we know this is difficult for you, and in Zoe's sweet loving manner—" she lifted a daring eyebrow at Zoe when she snorted again "—she's offering support. *We're* offering support."

Delia let her gaze fall back to Jacob. "Okay. I might be a *little* nervous." She straightened and shot Zoe a look. "But I'm not scared, so just zip it or I'll make you do *my* chores for a change. I doubt you'd last long making beds."

Zoe grinned and swung an arm around Delia's shoulders. "Let's go greet our baby brother, okay?"

"Together," Maddie said, hugging them both.

Grateful for their love and support, Delia opened the front door—just in time to see who else got out of Ty's truck.

Cade.

And damn her traitorous heart, it gave a leap of gladness.

"It's simple once you get the hang of it," Delia said to Jacob as she assisted him into the saddle.

"You just hold on here." She handed him the reins and smiled up into his nervous-but-trying-to-be-cool face. "How does it feel?"

He lifted a shoulder, silent and slightly sullen.

"Okay, good." Delia said, ignoring the attitude. She'd been the queen of attitude growing up, so she figured she could deal with it, knowing it was the only way he felt comfortable communicating for now.

Ty had saddled two horses so that she could take Jacob out on a ride. He'd offered to go with them, as had Zoe, but Delia wanted to do this alone the first time.

However, she couldn't help but wish Jacob had picked something else for his first adventure on the Triple M. She also wished he'd let go of some of his resentment.

And yet he'd wanted to come.

"Let's go," she said, hoisting herself into Betsy's saddle. "We'll stick to the trails and keep to a walk."

"Why?"

"Because we're both beginners."

Disappointment filled his face. "You're a beginner, too?"

"Well…" It'd never been easy to admit her shortcomings. How could she tell him she was really a city girl, more accustomed to lights and sirens than the musical silence of the wilderness? All her own self-doubts threatened to drown her, but she managed to shove them aside. "Yes, I'm a beginner, but together we—"

"I wanna go with someone who knows what they're doing."

"I'd probably want the same thing."

Both Delia and Jacob turned at the sound of Cade's voice, and Cade had to smile at their twin looks of irritation. Like brother, like sister, he thought, pushing away from the fence and moving closer. "How's it going, Jacob?"

"Fine." Jacob eyed Cade's faded jeans, blue chambray shirt and scuffed boots. "You look like a cowboy," he said, smiling.

"Do I?" Cade had avoided meeting Delia's gaze, but he did so now, and felt the usual punch to his system, not because of her beauty, but because something passed between them, something he was attempting to ignore. "How about some company?" he asked her.

"Can you teach me to gallop?" Jacob asked. "Can you?"

Delia's face was unreadable; she was good at keeping herself closed off. Too good. But he thought he knew how she felt about him coming along.

She didn't want him.

"'Cause I want to learn to race," Jacob said.

Oh, boy. Tommy had been five when he'd died, and that had been eight years ago, but it felt like only yesterday he'd heard that whiny tone. Cade's long-forgotten and rusty father skills resurfaced. So did a rush of pain at his loss.

"You can't race until you learn what you're doing, Ace. And for starters, you've got to keep your feet in the stirrups."

Jacob blushed and muttered, "I didn't know. And anyway, she's just a beginner too." He tossed his head toward Delia.

Delia's hat shielded a good part of her face, but Cade had no trouble detecting how hurt she was by Jacob's not-too-subtle criticism.

"She's your sister and the one who invited you here," Cade said carefully but with an unmistakable warning. He remembered this, too, having to correct and discipline. It wasn't his place here, and as a result, he had no trouble sensing Delia's unhappiness at both Jacob's tone and his own interference.

Damn, he shouldn't have come back. Hadn't wanted to come back.

Liar.

But there was something about these hurting, proud siblings that drew him. The urge to help them was stronger than his own urge to run. "Are you unhappy here already?" he asked Jacob.

The boy shot a quick look at Delia. "No."

"You sure?"

"I'm sure."

"Okay, just checking. Look, Jacob, it's good to communicate and tell people how you feel, but it's not good to hurt people with words. Do you understand?''

Jacob stole another peek at Delia. "Yeah," he responded.

"Because if you'd rather, we can arrange for you to fly back to Southern California."

"Cade," Delia said quietly.

He reached out and settled a hand at the base of her spine, his arm resting on her saddle, and felt her instinctive reaction in the tightening of her muscles. He left his hand on her, feeling his own tightening, as well. "So what's it going to be, Jacob?"

The boy stared at the brilliant blue sky, dotted with huge puffy clouds. "Stay," he said quietly. Then he shocked Cade by looking straight at Delia. "I want to stay. With you."

Delia blinked, for a moment incapable of hiding her surprise. Clearly touched, she said huskily, "You can stay for as long as you want."

Cade looked at Jacob steadily, until the boy's shoulders sagged. "I'm sorry," he mumbled. "I didn't mean to be rude."

"I know," Delia told him. "We're still getting used to each other, aren't we? I won't apologize for being a beginner, but maybe we can learn to ride together."

He sent her a cheeky smile. "Can we learn from Cade?"

Delia met Cade's eyes and saw a whole host of

things there, things he didn't know what to do with.

"Yes," she answered Jacob, still looking into Cade's eyes. "I imagine there's a lot we can learn from Cade."

Cade found himself staring right back, absorbing her silent gratitude, her affection.

Jacob urged his horse forward at a slow walk.

Delia hesitated, then said softly for Cade's ears only. "You're so good with him. As if..."

As if he knew what he was doing?

He *did* know, or once upon a time he'd known. "I understand kids," was all he managed to say.

She sent him a warm sweet smile, and he was helpless to hold back his own.

Chapter 9

They took Jacob on a ride through the hills behind the ranch. The light snow from the night before hadn't stuck, but the ground was stiff with frost. With it crunching beneath their feet and the hush of the oncoming winter, they were in their own world.

With each mile, more of Jacob's bad attitude faded and more of the real Delia showed. Cade held himself back, afraid that being with this woman who'd become so special to him and with the boy who was rapidly becoming special would be painful.

After all, it should remind him of a life he'd had long ago, and in some ways it did.

But Delia wasn't his wife, and Jacob wasn't his son.

And much as he didn't want to admit it, he felt more joy than pain.

He reined in his horse, and both Delia and Jacob came to a stop behind him. "Ready for that run now?" he asked Jacob, whose face lit up before he remembered to play it cool.

"If you want," he said with his characteristic one-shouldered shrug.

Delia opened her mouth, and Cade was certain she was about to veto the idea. Before she could, he scooped the boy onto his horse and settled him in front. Jacob immediately stiffened away from the physical contact, but Cade just smiled. That would change, and soon. He handed Jacob's reins to Delia, who gave him a long look.

"What are you doing?"

"He wants to gallop," Cade said simply, as if he didn't suddenly feel the need to run hard and fast and furious himself.

Delia's eyes narrowed. She was on to him, no doubt. "Be careful."

"Always. Hold on," he whispered to Jacob, slipping an arm around his waist. Then he let the horse have its way, and they took off at a fast clip across a wide meadow.

Jacob held himself stiff for exactly one second before he gave in. He clutched the arm Cade had around him, but laughed joyously as the wind whipped icily against their faces.

"Good?" Cade shouted.

"The best," Jacob shouted back with a wide grin. "More!"

Cade gave it, and for a few short glorious moments horse, boy and man ran free as the wind. It felt inconceivably...right. At the end of the meadow, Cade brought the horse to a stop. Jacob straightened away from him immediately, but turned his head to look at Cade, his eyes sparkling. "I want to do that on my own horse. Can I?"

"Soon." Cade laughed, reaching forward to ruffle the kid's hair in a gesture that felt as natural as breathing. God, he'd forgotten how good it felt to be with a kid, how kids smelled like youth and innocence, how they laughed with abandon, how everything they felt they wore on their sleeve. "But definitely not today. Delia would skin me alive if I got you injured on your first day here."

They both turned to look for her. She was still on her horse, leading Jacob's, slowly making her way toward them.

"She's still far enough away..." Jacob looked at him hopefully, making Cade laugh again.

"Not a chance. I'm not risking my stay here for another joy ride. Or my dinner. Maddie's cooking her pot roast, and in case you're wondering, it's to die for." Plus, he had no problem making out Delia's anxious gaze as she came closer. "If I haven't risked it already," Cade muttered.

But as she came up to them, she smiled, mostly in response to Jacob's grin, Cade thought. "Fun?"

"Yeah." Jacob looked at Cade, and there was

no mistaking the adoration there. "He's going to teach me to ride like he does."

"You'll have to come back to do that," Delia said, only her eyes betraying how important Jacob's response was to her. "Think you'll want to?"

Jacob reached down and stroked the horse's neck. The animal gave a huff of pleasure. "Yeah. I want to come back."

Delia slid off her horse, and from her natural grace and ease of movement, no one would have guessed how new to riding she was. Then her horse snorted and Delia leaped back, eyes wide.

No one but me, Cade silently corrected, biting back a smile.

She moved toward Cade's horse and looked up into Jacob's eyes. "I'm hoping someday you'll want to come here and…well, maybe stay."

"You mean, *live* here with you?"

Again, only her eyes gave away her emotion. "Yeah."

Jacob scratched his head and looked puzzled. "I don't know."

Delia merely nodded. But Cade caught her hard swallow and the stricken flash in her eyes, and he nearly reached for her, but then Jacob spoke again.

"I used to not have anyone to live with," he said, "you know, after my mom died. Now all of a sudden, everyone wants me to live with them."

"Everyone? Like who?"

"Edna," Jacob said. "You. And Scott."

"Scott?" Delia repeated with more than a little surprise. "Scott wants you to live with him?"

"He said it was going to be up to the judge, but if I wanted, I could tell the judge who I wanted to live with most." Confusion flickered in his eyes. "I thought living with Scott would be great. He's got a puppy, and he said it could be mine."

"But now…you're mixed up?" Delia asked gently.

Jacob shrugged again. "A little."

"I'd be confused, too," Delia said. "So many choices. Why don't you just think about it for a while, okay? No one is asking you to make any decision right now. Don't feel rushed."

"Okay."

Delia smiled at Jacob, and Cade smiled at her, willing his support and affection into her hurting heart. She shocked him by returning that smile.

Jacob pointed to a large rock on the bluff overlooking the river. "Can we go fast again? Just to the rock?"

Delia nodded, and with her permission, Cade held Jacob tightly and let the wind take them.

Afterward, Maddie coaxed Jacob into the house with the promise of chocolate-chip cookies, and he didn't hesitate.

Which left Cade and Delia alone, still on their horses, in front of the house.

"Scott wants him," Delia repeated dully, staring off into space.

Cade knew it wasn't all that uncommon for so-cial workers to take in one or more foster kids themselves. He had a friend who ran the child-welfare service in Arizona, and she took in kids all the time.

"Why didn't he tell me?" Delia asked.

"I don't know, but it makes me wonder," Cade said.

"Which brings me to something else I've been wondering about." She turned and looked right at him. "Why did you come back?"

He sighed, wishing they didn't have to do this. He didn't want to hurt her any more than she'd already been hurt. "You were right about your fa-ther. He wasn't a cop. There's no record of him on the force."

"You could have told me that on the tele-phone," Delia responded.

Because he was well aware of that fact, and an-noyed and confused about it, he ignored her words. "Also, Ethan Constance used different names. I've tracked down at least five of them so far."

"But not Eddie Kitze?"

"Not yet, but that doesn't mean anything. I'll find him, Delia."

Her eyes were still on his, cool and steady. "You could have told me that over the phone, too."

"And could I have helped you with Jacob over the phone?"

At her desolate expression, he swore, shoved a

hand through his hair and took a deep breath. "I'm sorry, but you're driving me insane, you know that?"

"Exactly my point in asking why you came back."

"I didn't intend to. I went to New York, tracking down someone on another case, and every single woman I looked at, I...I saw you. You, dammit, and I've got to tell you, I didn't like it."

She had the nerve to look amused, if slightly unsettled.

"After New York I hit Florida, for what should have been a nice cozy little break. I was lying on the beach and listening to the surf, thinking life was pretty good. I'd just closed two big cases and was getting closer to tracking your father and solving Constance's case. Should have been a real personal triumph for me, and all I could think about was the snow, these Idaho peaks, the Triple M...and you, dammit. You. Your cool smile and hot eyes. Your laugh. The way you make me want..." *Want to live again.*

The thought was beginning to haunt him.

Turning his horse away, he swore again and gazed into the distance, unable to come to terms with everything he was feeling.

"Want what?" she whispered.

"I doubt you really want to know." He drew in a deep breath. "It's fairly involved."

"Oh, and I can't handle 'involved'?"

"Not this kind of involved."

"Well, that's interesting coming from a man who can't stay in one spot long enough to grow roots."

He looked at her. "Isn't that like the pot calling the kettle black?"

"I have a home."

"Yes, a home. But you won't share feelings and emotions, not when they run deep enough to make you hurt."

She stared at him, then slipped off Betsy and started to lead her toward the barn. At the last moment she turned back. "I owe you a thank-you. I'll never forget how you helped me with Jacob. How you helped me gain access to his heart."

"That was you, Delia, not me."

"Maybe I could have done it without you, but it would have taken longer. You have a way with him, and I'm grateful."

"I don't want your gratitude."

"I can see that. So go away, Cade. Go away and stay there this time."

"You don't know how much I want to do just that, but I can't." He dismounted, as well, and moved close to her, close enough to see her chest rise and fall with her uneven breathing, close enough to see the pain in her eyes, pain he'd put there. "You asked me about my past, and I didn't answer you."

She shrugged as if it didn't matter, but he knew better. "I was married," he said quietly, moderately satisfied to see her shock. "I had a son. They…both died."

"Oh…oh, Cade." Her eyes filled with sorrow.

"It was a long time ago," he said quickly to smother her pity. "Eight years."

"How?"

In her eyes was so much compassion and sympathy he nearly choked on it. "It was my fault." He moistened suddenly dry lips, but there was nothing he could do about the lump in his throat. He never talked about this, never, but he would now. "I worked a lot, as an attorney. Lisa was always after me to take a vacation, but I was too busy becoming a somebody." His mouth twisted bitterly. "God, I was so selfish back then it kills me even to think about it." Wearily he rubbed his temples, and when he felt her hand on his back, offering a comfort he didn't deserve, he went absolutely still.

Purposely he moved away from her hand and ignored the look of hurt on her face.

"What happened?" she asked.

"I finally agreed to get away. We went to Colorado, just the three of us, but I got called back to L.A. to testify on a case."

"Did you go?"

"I remember how upset Lisa was at the call. She wanted me to spend more time with her and Tommy, and she reminded me I'd promised not to work. But I still left and…and I didn't get back when I promised I would."

"What happened?"

"She and Tommy went on a drive without me, hoping to explore a little bit. Her Jeep broke down out in the middle of nowhere, in a sudden winter storm. They froze to death."

"Oh, God, Cade. I'm so sorry." She lifted a clear far-too-compassionate gaze up to his. "But how is that your fault?"

How was that his fault? How could she even ask? "I wasn't there," he said, his self-fury nearly choking him. "And I should have been."

"So you could have died, as well? Oh, Cade—"

"No. No, don't say anything. Since then, I haven't been able to…settle in one spot for long. I just…" He was horrified at how his voice cracked.

"I just wanted you to know."

"It wasn't your fault," she said vehemently. "You couldn't have known what would happen."

"It *was* my fault. Always will be. But that's not why I told you." He put his hands on her shoulders, let them slide up her throat to cup her face. "I told you because if things were different, if I could settle down, I'd want to do it right here, close to you, close to Jacob and your sisters, and be a part of your life."

Delia's voice was very soft, her eyes very bright. "I think I just might like that, Cade McKnight."

"But I can't, Delia. God, I just…can't."

"I know," she whispered, and because he couldn't handle all he saw in her eyes, he took the horses and walked away.

* * *

Cade left that afternoon. He had to. The emotional roller coaster his life had become was unbearable.

Only he didn't count on it to be unbearable from wherever he was.

In his Boise office, he worked diligently at his computer. Mostly to keep his mind occupied, but also because something about Jacob's revelation regarding Scott's desire for custody seemed off.

Scott Felton was an exemplary social worker and he had the accolades to prove it. To his credit, he'd also taken kids into his own home before. He shared a house with his sister, also a social worker, and they were licensed to house kids. Many times over past few years, they'd taken in kids no one else could or would.

But that didn't ease Cade's instinctive feeling something wasn't right.

Calling in several markers, Cade made some phone calls and put out feelers. It all could be on the up-and-up, but he sincerely doubted that.

While he was at it, he continued his trace on Eddie Kitze, determined that if he couldn't give Delia a future, he could at least give her back her past.

"I think the visit was a hit— Ouch!" Zoe wailed, yanking her hand out of Delia's.

"You have a hangnail," Delia said, calmly

reaching for Zoe's hand. She was attempting to give her a manicure. "Come back here."

"No way, that hurt."

Delia laughed. "You work from sunup to sundown outside in the harsh sun. You get splinters, you get rudely thrown off horses, you slam your fingers in the barn door—"

"One time," Zoe interrupted. "I slammed my finger in the door one time, and technically that doesn't count because it was the wind's fault. And as for the horses, I never get thrown off."

"My point is," Delia said evenly, taking back Zoe's resistant hand, "that surely you can handle one little manicure."

Zoe's eyes narrowed. "You don't give a hoot about my nails. You're trying to take your mind off something. Is it sweet little Jacob or hot sexy Cade?"

"As if I would waste one second on that man."

"Cade," Zoe corrected with a laugh. "His name is Cade."

"Whatever."

"Delia. Come on, tell me." All joking was set aside as her sister looked at her in earnest. "Please, talk to me."

"I'm sorry. God, you're right, it's stupid to torture you. I mean, polish is a complete waste on those nails."

"Exactly." Zoe pulled her work-roughened hands back with relief and studied her sister. "You're worrying me, Dee. You're keeping everything inside. It's not good for you, remember? You told me that when I fell in love with Ty and couldn't accept it. You and Maddie hounded me until I finally opened up, and if I hadn't, I would have blown up." Reaching out, she squeezed Delia's hands. "You're going to blow up, Delia, I can feel it. So spill it."

"I am not going to blow up." But wasn't she? Couldn't she feel the pressure building slowly but inexorably?

"Then it's about Jacob? I mean Cade is fantastic, more than fantastic, but you're right, you'd never let a man get to you."

Delia nearly laughed, but it would have been hysterical. No, tough independent Delia would never let a man get to her.

And pigs could fly.

"Jacob is terrific," Zoe said softly. "And Edna seemed to accept his coming here as inevitable. It'll happen, Delia."

She could only hope. But Delia still had serious doubts, and since she'd lied to her sisters, neglecting to tell them how likely it was that she wasn't going to be worthy in the judge's eyes, she had no one to blame but herself for having to handle this alone.

Not all alone, a little voice inside her said. *Cade has been there for you since this ordeal began.* Without words he'd made it clear she could always lean on him, no matter where he was or what was between them.

Well, dammit, she wanted to lean on him right now, and didn't know how to ask.

Later that evening, Delia was alone in her room with nothing but her needle and thread for company. She loved sewing, it was relaxing. Filled with pleasure at the sight of Zoe's wedding gown spread before her, Delia smiled and hummed to herself as she handstitched lace to silk. There'd been no new snow, and she hadn't seen a spider in days. Things were as good as they could get.

Until the soft knock came at her door. She knew it was Cade, somehow she just knew, and for a moment her entire body went warm and still.

"Delia."

His voice did it to her every single time, rendered her…well, stupid. She managed to stand but didn't open the door. The handle turned, then he was there—tall, forceful, darkly handsome…and gazing at her as if she was the only woman on earth.

For a moment she let herself believe that. Then she took a second look and saw that his big body was tense, his eyes dark with concern and barely contained anger.

"What?" she whispered. "What is it?"

Now those eyes filled with something else. Regret. And she braced herself.

"Delia, Scott is up to his eyeballs in debt."

Chapter 10

Delia couldn't afford to go to Los Angeles, not when she'd gone twice already and planned to go again for the custody hearing. But then Cade had shown up at the ranch with his shocking news.

Cade hadn't just stumbled on the information regarding Scott's financial situation. It'd taken a lot of digging, so while it ostensibly had nothing to do with Jacob, they could be certain Scott was up to something. She had no idea what, but if he owed so much and if Jacob's inheritance was as big as Edna had led her to believe, Delia had a big problem.

First, Scott had never mentioned he wanted custody of Jacob. Why would he hide it from her? Since she'd come into the picture rather late, and for a long time there had been no one to take Jacob, it wouldn't have been so odd for Scott to step forward. That he hadn't seemed strange.

Second, and most disturbing, if Scott indeed managed to hide his financial trouble from the courts and won custody of Jacob, all her brother's money would be in Scott's control.

Coincidental? Maybe not. With all the possessiveness and protectiveness of a mother bear, she intended to watch out for her baby brother, no matter what.

In light of that, her poor credit card could take this last flight, or so she hoped, but it would certainly max out soon and she'd be left with nothing in case of emergency.

Which made her laugh. An emergency.

What else could happen?

"I paid for the tickets already," Cade told her. It was morning and they were on their way to the airport.

Her sisters had offered her money, too, when neither of them could afford this any more than she could. The ranch was on its way to solvency, but they were still deeply in the red. They wouldn't even begin to recoup until summer, when business should pick up.

"No." Delia refused to be a charity case, as she had for most of her life. "No, thank you," she said firmly, staring out the car window and watching the stark white landscape fly by. "I pay my own way."

"It's too late." He spoke mildly, but there was steel in his voice. "I already arranged it."

"Cade—"

"Let me do this, Delia." His large hands flexed on the steering wheel and he flashed her a quick burning look before returning his gaze to the road. "It's the least I can do."

Why? she wondered.

Because he refused to give her what she really wanted, which had nothing to do with his wallet? The thought stopped her cold. All her life she'd told herself she wanted security. And all her life she'd told herself that meant a certain social status. Financial stability. She'd even joked about finding her prince.

But that made her a fortune hunter and no better than her own unsympathetic mother.

She hated that thought. *She was like her own mother.*

No, she reminded herself, she was finding that wasn't true at all. She'd thought she wanted those things, but in the end, it had nothing to do with money. It was about security of the heart.

It was a hell of a time to realize that, when she wanted so much more than Cade could give. And knowing his past, she certainly couldn't blame him for his inability to give it. He'd loved his wife and child with all his heart, and now that heart was broken, without room for more love.

And that was okay.

No, that was a lie, too, a painful one. She might have hidden a lot of truths from her sisters, but with herself she'd always been brutally honest. And what she wanted from Cade scared her to death.

Everything about him scared her to death, and because of that, she wanted to fight him on the money issue. She *needed* to fight him, but she was exhausted from their last run of guests and the lack of sleep she'd experienced from thinking too much. "I'm paying you back," she said stubbornly.

Cade's jaw tightened, but he said nothing until they were on the plane.

When they'd hit full altitude, he turned toward her, put his hands on either armrest so that she was caged in by him and leaned close. "How long are you going to pull this 'I'm too strong to need you' act?"

Her stomach fell, and it had nothing to do with the altitude. "I *don't* need you."

His response was a low obscenity. "You're good to go, right, Delia? Strong enough to take on the world, screw those who care about you."

"Cade—"

"How long until you break down and admit that this is all too much for one person to handle and that it's okay to lean on someone?"

"Who would I lean on?" she asked in a polite voice so he wouldn't know how deeply he'd cut.

She *was* strong enough, damn him. She leveled him with a look that would have withered any other male. Not Cade, who just met her gaze evenly. Steadily. Patiently.

"Your sisters for starters," he suggested.

With a huge sigh, she broke eye contact. "I can't," she mumbled, feeling the shame heat her face.

"Why the hell not?"

She studied the cloud formation.

"Delia."

"Because."

"Because why?"

"Because I lied to them about the trouble I might have getting custody, okay? I couldn't stand the thought of failure or the fact that I've made nothing of my life, so much so that I couldn't even get custody of my own brother."

"Oh, Delia." With a gentleness that nearly broke her, he forced her to look at him. "You aren't looking at yourself very clearly if you honestly believe that."

"You're the one with rose-colored glasses here, Cade."

"You're the most amazing woman. I wish you could see you the way I do."

Embarrassed, she scoffed and tried to look away, but he held her, and in his touch she found the oddest thing. Comfort. In his voice she found honesty and an affection that made her swallow hard. "How do you see me?"

"As a woman strong and capable, yet warm and full of passion for life. You're incredible, Delia."

She turned away, she had to, for he'd touched her deeply, and embarrassed her, too.

"No, listen to me," he said urgently. "I know your life hasn't been easy, you've certainly never been given any advantages, and yet look at you. By sheer grit and hard work, you've made a life for yourself and your sisters. You run a guest ranch, for God's sake. You're still in control, Delia. You can do this."

"Can I?" she whispered.

"Yeah. Oh, yeah." His voice was strong and sure. It was full of a pride that made her want to believe him just to prove herself worthy of his trust.

"Delia…what about me?" His gaze held hers, his fingers stroked her cheek. "During those times when you can't always be strong, when you need someone, why can't you come to me?"

"I think that's pretty obvious, considering you're the one who runs as fast as he can every time we get too close."

The golden specks in his eyes danced with a sudden heat. "I'm not running now," he whispered.

"Running now would be detrimental to your health," she said, glancing outside. But damn him, she was breathless. Just one touch and she was leaning toward him, oblivious to the passengers around them, hoping, craving, nearly begging for his mouth to meet hers.

"Delia," he said. Just that, just her name on a little sigh as he kissed her lightly. "I think I have a problem." His mouth touched hers again. *"You."*

That had her spine stiffening, even as her mouth tingled from his kiss. "I'm no one's problem. And I'm not going to fall apart. I don't ever fall apart." Turning away, she stared out the window, watching her mountains vanish as she headed back to her city.

The man beside her remained silent as she watched her two worlds mesh.

They drove directly to Scott's office, but Cade could think of little else other than Delia.

She was an enigma, cool, sophisticated, elegant. And yet much of that was just a front for the woman beneath, the woman he was beginning to know better than he'd ever intended.

She had a heart of gold, though she'd probably freeze him over with one hard gaze if he dared to tell her so. She was the strongest, most compassionate, most vulnerable woman he'd ever met.

And he wanted her with everything he had.

What a mess. He'd told himself he'd never again open up his heart, not after suffering the loss of his precious family for eight long years.

Eight long years.

But didn't he, maybe just a little, deserve some happiness?

Delia didn't say a word as they were ushered into Scott's office.

He was on the phone when they entered, and though Scott didn't seem pleased to see them, he hung up and smiled politely. "Hello."

"You haven't been honest with me," Delia said calmly before Cade could speak. "You want custody of Jacob and you never told me."

"Why should I have?" He folded his hands and watched her with unreadable eyes. "You showed up out of the blue wanting Jacob. I couldn't be expected to trust that you were who you said you were."

"I showed up out of the blue," Delia responded, "because I didn't know Jacob existed until Cade started researching my past for the Triple M. And once I did come into the picture, you knew exactly who I was. You had me checked out before you approved visitation with Jacob."

"Checking you out is procedure."

"And yet the question remains," Cade said. "Why didn't you mention you wanted custody?"

"It was never a secret," Scott insisted. "Jacob is—was—completely alone. We didn't even have Edna in the picture then. We just…" He shrugged. "We bonded in a very strong way right from the beginning. He needed someone and he liked me, even trusted me. I decided to petition for custody, because I saw no problem with my taking him."

"But then you found Edna," Cade said. "Did you rescind your request for custody then?"

"Yes, we found Edna, who was blood-related and was willing and able to handle both the boy and his financial situation."

"So did you rescind the custody request?" Cade pressed, and Scott broke eye contact.

"No," he said without further explanation.

"Does Edna know?"

"Look, all along we've known Edna's just a temporary situation."

Cade wasn't buying that. "Because of her age?"

"Yes. She'd keep him, but it isn't her first choice."

"And your keeping Jacob had nothing to do with anything but your fondness for him?"

Scott's eyes narrowed. "What are you getting at?"

"It's just a question."

"I don't think I like the implication."

"I haven't implied anything. Yet. But there is the matter of your considerable debt," Cade said.

Scott went still.

"Stock-market problems, Scott? Or maybe drugs?"

"I've never done drugs. I take care of children, for God's sake," Scott said furiously.

"Gambling, then?"

"That's none of your business. I don't know how you could have found out."

"If I did, so will the court. You must realize you'll be investigated if you're going for custody."

"I'm already approved for foster care—I have been for years. Again, this is none of your business."

"No, but it's Jacob's," Cade said. "He has a sizable inheritance."

"That money is protected by his trust fund."

"And accessible to Jacob's guardian."

Scott rose. "I'd like both of you to leave now."

"I'm sure you would," Cade said, rising, too, and reaching for Delia's hand. He was shocked to feel it tremble before she turned up her palm to lock their fingers.

"This isn't over," she said to Scott.

"I think it is," he replied.

"Have you turned in your report to the judge yet?" Cade asked.

Scott's body couldn't have gotten tenser. His phone rang but he ignored it. "No."

Cade pulled Delia to the door. "Recommend Delia," he suggested. "Edna's only helping out of the goodness of her heart. There's no reason for anyone else to take Jacob when his own sister wants him."

"Unless that sister isn't qualified."

"I'm perfectly qualified," Delia said proudly. "And don't you dare throw the size of my bank account into my face, not ever again. You're worse off than I am, and if I have to, I'll make sure the judge knows it."

She was glorious under pressure, Cade thought, watching her and experiencing feelings so strong he nearly staggered. No matter what life threw at her, she held up, when anyone else might have given up. "What's it going to be, Scott?"

But the phone rang again, and Scott turned his back on them to answer it. Delia tugged Cade out of the office.

They didn't speak until they were outside the tall building, standing on a small patch of grass in front of the parking lot, staring into the hot humid day.

"He's not going to give up, is he?" Delia asked dully. She'd let go of Cade's hand the moment they'd left Scott's office, but he took it again now.

"We scared him," he said. "I doubt he'll dare mess with you now."

"But what if he still looks better to the judge?"

The vulnerability she'd never really allowed him to see before shone through now, and it tugged at him hard. "We make sure the judge knows about his debts. Today. We send him the information we have on Scott and let Scott sink himself. Besides, by the custody-hearing date, I'm hoping we'll have proof you're the heir and you'll have your sisters and Ty to back you up. Come on, honey, let's go surprise Jacob and take him out for his favorite pizza."

Delia went still at the endearment that had slipped so effortlessly off his tongue. She'd never liked it when a man called her such things. She'd never felt it honest, because in truth, she'd never allowed herself to be another man's "honey" or anything remotely close.

But hearing Cade's deep warm voice call her "honey," well, it seemed another matter entirely. And without meaning to, she looked up at him with all of her heart in her eyes.

In response, he whispered her name as he softly touched her face, brushed her hair off her cheek.

"I've been trying to keep this simple between us," she said. "And yet what I feel for you isn't simple at all." His gaze met hers and she smiled bemusedly. "I don't want to feel it, you don't want to feel it, either, so why won't it just go away and leave us alone?"

His eyes were serious as he skimmed her jaw with one calloused palm. "I haven't a clue. Come here, Delia."

They were completely alone in the tiny park. Her eyes never left his as she did what he asked and stepped closer.

"This is one of the moments when maybe we could share strength. Sort of double it up. What do you think?"

"Why do you need to be strong? This is my problem, right?"

He shook his head. "No, you're not alone, remember? *Our* problem. And I need your strength because just being with you makes me feel a bit weak. Help me out here, could you?"

He was teasing her, of course. He didn't need

her strength—he was strong enough for the both of them—but he thought he could help, he wanted to help, and suddenly she knew she was going to let him. Without hesitation she curled her arms around his neck at the same moment he wrapped his around her waist. Slowly they drifted closer and closer, till they were in an embrace that was as necessary as breathing.

"Damn, you feel good," he whispered in her ear, and when she settled her hips against his, she felt him harden. Not thinking, only reacting to the bolt of heat spiraling through her, she pressed herself to him, eliciting a deep-throated groan that vibrated from his chest to hers.

"Am I sharing enough strength?" she asked shakily, trying to laugh off all this unbearable heat between them, because if she didn't, she might drown in it.

He didn't return the laugh, but nudged himself closer against her. She became lost in the feel of him, then the taste of him when he bent to take her mouth in a deep wet kiss that made her forget Jacob, forget Scott, forget that they were standing in a public place, locked in each other's arms.

However, reality intruded a few seconds later when a car raced by them. And the reality was, they were two people who couldn't seem to stay away from each other and yet were not able to let go of the demons of their past enough to be together.

For just a moment, a weak moment, pressed safe

and warm against his lean muscular body, Delia couldn't remember why he couldn't be "the One," and she thought maybe, just maybe, he'd forgotten why she couldn't be, too.

He broke off the kiss and let out a groan, dropping his forehead to hers as his chest jerked with his ragged breathing. "The more you share, the weaker I get," he muttered in her ear.

The power of that, of making this incredible male tremble, went straight to her head. She couldn't hold back her satisfied little smile, and he had to return it.

"In fact," he said, his voice still rough with desire, "if you share any more, I am going to drop right here on the ground. We'd better go." But he took another second to slide his big hands down her spine to briefly cup her bottom. "Before I forget that we're standing out in public and drag you down to that bench over there."

Because she couldn't help herself, she gave one last arch toward him, watching his eyes darken all the more. "Oh, that helps," he muttered. "Delia—"

"I know." Suddenly cold, she pulled away. She'd nearly forgotten that he didn't want this between them.

Ignoring the heartache, she walked away from him and got into the car.

Chapter 11

"Tell us everything about your visit with Jacob," Maddie demanded that next night.

The three foster sisters were in the hot tub. Ty had just gone into the kitchen to muster up a snack.

"Well, let's see..." Delia leaned back against the warm tile to stare up into the cloudy night. An occasional snowflake fell, cooling her steaming skin, as she remembered the visit to Scott's office and the subsequent letter she and Cade had drafted to the authorities, outlining Scott's financial problems. She could only hope it worked. "He creamed me in basketball and then I creamed him in a serious card game of war."

"You probably cheated," Zoe said, and Delia laughed.

"I never cheat. You're confusing me with you."

"You calling me a cheater?"

"Girls, girls," Maddie said with a dramatic sigh, and they all laughed again.

"So was it heaven?" Maddie asked.

"Yeah." Delia smiled, though it was a bitter-sweet one. "Then hell when I had to leave him. He asked me when he could come back here and I promised him as soon as possible."

"How perfect," Maddie said, smiling brilliantly. "He wants to come back to us."

"And not just for a visit." Delia remembered how Jacob had stood there, hands jammed into his pockets, as he'd muttered something she couldn't quite catch. When she'd asked him to repeat it, he'd gone red in the face but had looked right at her.

"Maybe I could," he'd said, "you know, come stay with you. Like…live there. Maybe. Some-time."

He'd spoken casually, but with his heart on his sleeve, and Delia's chest had ached. "He wants to come live here," she said.

Zoe smiled in satisfaction at that. "He loves me."

Maddie splashed her sister. "He loved it here, with all of us. Oh, Dee, how wonderful! What did you tell him?"

Delia remembered how she'd knelt before him, her hands on his shoulders, her heart in her throat. "It's going to be up to the courts," she'd said, her joy nearly overwhelming her. It had been all she could do not to give in to the tears burning her eyes. But crying right then would have only confused him. "You're a very popular little boy, you know."

A smile had split his face. "I have options," he said. "Edna told me that. I pick you, Delia."

"I wish it was that easy," she managed. "But no matter what, you can come here as often as you want."

"With you and Maddie and Zoe?"

She'd smiled. "Yes."

"And Ty?" She could tell he'd had fun listing all the people in his life, people he would grow to love and care about. People who were his family.

"And Ty," she said.

"And Cade?"

Her smile had faltered then. "Cade doesn't live on the ranch, honey. He's just working on a case. When he's done, he'll be gone." Gone. For good. She could no longer think of it and muster up relief as she once had.

She didn't feel anything but a terrifying emptiness at the thought of Cade leaving her life for good. But she had no idea how to change their fate, so she did her best to ignore it.

To hide her roller-coaster emotions, she'd given Jacob a hug, and he'd only hesitated a second before hugging her back. Nothing had ever felt as good as having that scrawny squirming little boy in her arms.

"I told Jacob soon," she whispered now to her sisters. "Hopefully he'll come here and stay."

"So he wanted to know about Cade, too, huh?" Zoe watched Delia carefully, sinking deeper in the hot bubbling water. "You should know, Maddie and I have decided we love him."

"Good for you two."

"We can tell Cade loves it here with us," Maddie said, "in spite of himself."

"In spite of himself?" Delia narrowed her eyes. "What does that mean?"

"Delia." Maddie's voice was gentle. "I know the two of you have been circling each other like wild boars."

"Like boars in heat, more like," Zoe muttered, but wisely scooted back before Delia could splash her.

"I don't know what haunts him," Maddie said, "but something does. He's such a wonderful man. And we're so shorthanded. We were thinking..."

"That he belongs," Zoe finished bluntly. "We have more than enough room for him to have his office here if he wants, and frankly, he's got amazing know-all about this winter stuff. He's not busy full-time with his cases, and he loves the wilderness. He could take guests out on treks with horses or snowmobiles."

Delia rose and climbed out of the tub, immediately missing the warmth of the water. "No."

"Delia—"

"No," she said more firmly. "He won't want

to. My God, are you kidding?'' She managed a laugh because the thought of having Cade in front of her all the time, looking rugged and tough, and rangy and sexy every single day, but at the same time not really being able to have him… It would break her heart, and that simply couldn't be allowed to happen. ''No,'' she said again, and wrapped a towel around herself.

''Honey, wait—'' Maddie rose from the tub, too, and with a delicate shiver she approached Delia. ''If there's nothing between you and Cade—''

''There's not.''

''Then why are you so upset? He hasn't hurt you, or—''

''No.'' Delia gritted her teeth against Maddie's worry, because she hated causing Maddie anything but happiness. ''I'm sorry, it's just that I know you're right. I know Cade likes to be wild and free because it helps him avoid the fact he doesn't have a real home, and I even know why he does it, and while I feel terrible about it, I just don't know if I…if I can handle having him here.''

''You can handle anything,'' Zoe reminded her quietly. ''Which is why it's shocking to watch you run from this, to completely ignore what's happening between you and that man. That wonderful man, who's obviously been as hurt by life as we have. We have the advantage, though—we have a new start. Come on, Dee, don't you think he deserves the same? For once we have the upper hand, the ability to help others, instead of accepting what others can do for us. I can't believe you aren't willing to see that.''

"Zoe.'' A frown curved Maddie's mouth. "Don't be so hard on her.''

Delia closed her eyes. "No, Maddie, she's right.'' Her selfishness and all the things she hadn't told her sisters filled her with shame. They were both so honest, so open and willing to love and accept, and she'd lied to them by not admitting her custody troubles, by not admitting how she really felt about Cade, by holding herself back from them, when they never would have done that to her. "I think…I think I just need to get some sleep,'' she whispered.

But when she'd escaped to her bed, away from her sisters concerned gazes, there was no sleep to be found.

At dawn's light Delia had given up on the sweet escape of sleep. She'd gotten up, pulled on her clothes and gone outside.

Now she stood on the bank of the Salmon River, with the Triple M Guest Ranch at her back and the early-morning autumn sun on her face. The view was spectacular, but all she could see was her brother's hopeful expression.

She couldn't fail him.

Walking back to the house, the frozen ground crunched beneath her boots. Her breath crystallized in front of her face.

The mountains were white and brown. The

meadow was white and brown. But the sky and the river were a brilliant blue. The trees provided the green. And with the two red barns and the wood fencing throughout, the place could have been a postcard, it was so lovely. The colors were so bright, so clear, Delia expected to see them run together as if the whole thing was a painting.

Instead, she watched as a man left the ranch house and walked toward the barn. He was tall, with a confident stride she'd recognize anywhere.

Cade.

Her eyes narrowed. She hadn't known he was here. He must have arrived either very late last night or early this morning.

Without a hat, his dark hair was whipped by the wind. His broad shoulders were slightly hunched against the cold, his hands shoved in his pockets. From this distance, she couldn't see clearly, couldn't read his expression, but she had no problem sensing his unhappiness.

Dammit. She didn't want to wonder about that, didn't want to wonder if it was the memories of his family or the fact that for now he was tied here when he didn't want to be.

Or maybe it was *her* causing his misery.

Delia sighed. She wasn't one to sit around and let life take her for a ride. Which meant she needed to go talk to him. Needed to make sure…

Another unladylike oath left her lips, because she was lying to herself, looking for excuses to go see the man who fascinated her, who took up too much of her thoughts.

By the time she got to the barn, it was empty. The far door was open to the chilly wind. She was halfway through when one of the horses stuck his head over the top of his stall and nudged her.

She had to laugh at her racing heart. "You stop that," she told the horse. "That's rude."

He just watched her with his dark baleful eyes.

"I suppose you've mistaken me for Zoe, who spoils you rotten with apples."

The horse lifted his upper lip and searched through her pockets until she stepped back out of his way. "Nothing, champ. Sorry." Ignoring his snort, she headed toward the back door.

Cade stood in the opening, his arms braced against the jamb, staring out into the white day, silent, his body fraught with tension.

She knew he'd heard her enter the barn. She also knew he must have witnessed her little chat with the horse, but he didn't so much as look her way.

"This is new," she said lightly, as if his rejection mattered in the least to her. "This letting me come to you. Usually you can't wait to eavesdrop—" She gasped when he whirled suddenly, grabbing her hips.

Before she could take another breath, he'd maneuvered her back against the barn wall, holding her there with his powerful body. "You," he said, his tone low and rough. She had no idea if he was accusing her of something or speaking in awe.

Given the dark look on his handsome face, she guessed it wasn't the latter. "Yes," she agreed, swallowing hard at the sensation of being sandwiched between the wall and Cade McKnight. "Me."

His hips pressed into hers, and his hands cupped her face so he could stare down into it. "Zoe and Maddie and Ty called me out here last night."

With him against her as he was, it was difficult to think. But finally his words sank in. "They…they did? The wedding isn't until next week."

"The ranch is full come tomorrow. Ten guests. They asked—no, demanded—I come help."

Delia's thoughts raced. She knew they were expecting a full house. She also knew they could handle it. Her sisters had done what they'd wanted last night—they'd called him to come here. "I…didn't know."

"I figured." His thumb played over her lower lip, making it tingle, and then her mouth opened of its own accord. His eyes darkened all the more, two midnight fathomless pools. "They want me to stick around. To set up my office in the house, and be part of the staff when I can."

Much as she wanted to concentrate on the sensations running through her body at his touch, it was impossible to ignore his words.

Because no matter what his mouth said, she could hear the awe, the fear, the indecision in his tone. And knew, no matter what she wanted, her sisters had done the right thing for Cade. "Are you going to do it?"

"I don't know." He stared over her head, as if picturing it. "I'd be taking guests out. We could explore the wilderness."

She knew that appealed to his sense of wanderlust. She couldn't blame him; it even appealed to her, the ultimate city girl. Another shock.

He blinked, as if bringing himself back, and sighed heavily. "That's not why I'm here, though. Delia…"

Right then she knew. She knew by the way his expression filled with regret, by the way he tightened his hold on her so she couldn't escape. "You have news about my father," she said in a completely normal voice.

"Yes."

It was going to be bad; she could feel it in every cell of her body. "Just tell me, Cade. I'm a big girl. What's the matter—Eddie's trail harder to trace than you thought?"

"No." His voice was filled with disgust. "I traced Eddie Kitze just fine."

"To…Ethan Freeman?" God, she had everything riding on this. With Scott playing his games, she needed something in her corner. Even knowing about his money troubles didn't totally appease her, because she had no idea if it would matter to the judge.

She needed to be heir, dammit. "Cade, tell me."

He glanced down and she did, too, seeing with

surprise that her hands were gripping the front of his shirt. He covered them with his own. "I found Eddie Kitze. He really existed, and he wasn't Ethan Freeman. He'd lied about being an undercover cop because he was a rich spoiled brat, out for a good time, slumming, as Dottie called it. He was a coward, afraid of his daddy's wrath and the loss of his inheritance."

"Okay." She wasn't Ethan Freeman's daughter. She wasn't heir. "How did you find out?"

"Paper trails. After we separated in Los Angeles, I went back to good old Dottie."

"And opened your wallet again," she guessed bitterly.

He didn't deny that, which only added to her misery. "She had some insight to your mother's life-style, which filled some of the holes."

"Such as why she dumped me? God, she must have been so angry when my father ditched her and left her saddled with a baby she never wanted."

"She wasn't angry, not then. Actually, she was thrilled, because it meant they were equals of a sort. But that was before she told him she was pregnant."

"He ditched her."

"He denied knowing her first. Her family disowned her, and by the time you were three, she was broke and pretty furious about it."

No wonder she'd left Delia at a foster home. She'd probably been reminded of her stupidity

every time she looked at her daughter. Delia gri-
maced and told herself enough of the self-pity.

She had Jacob to think of now—and no way to
guarantee custody.

Her eyes burned with that knowledge. Her throat
became so tight she couldn't have spoken her feelings if she'd wanted to.

And Cade's eyes were on her, dark and compassionate. "Delia," he whispered in a voice filled
with too much pity to take. "Sweetheart, I'm
sorry—"

"No," she whispered, flinching away when he
tried to touch her.

"You'll still get Jacob. You will."

"Yes," she said, not knowing if she was reas-
suring him or herself; either way she didn't believe
it. She was incredibly close to meltdown, closer
than she'd been in some time, and she couldn't
have him witness it, not when she wanted to be
strong. Needed to be strong. "I…I need to go."

"But—"

"I… Goodbye."

And she pushed away and ran from the barn,
hoping to make it somewhere private before the
tears swimming in her eyes fell.

Chapter 12

Cade stared after the quickly vanishing Delia. She wanted to be alone, she'd made that clear, but he wasn't convinced being alone was the best thing for her.

She seemed perfectly in control, but he knew that was what she wanted him to see, that beneath that mask of icy elegance was a woman close to shattering.

And why wouldn't she be? He'd just destroyed what she saw as her only hope to get her brother, though he didn't believe that to be true. It went deeper than that, though, which is what disturbed him.

Whether she admitted it or not, she had calculated her self-worth on her past. And discovering she'd come from two selfish strangers who couldn't care less about the tiny miracle of life they'd created had destroyed her.

It made her feel as though she was nothing, as though she deserved nothing, when in his opinion, she deserved the world. She certainly deserved to have someone love her. Her sisters did, but as hard as it was to believe, Cade wasn't quite certain that Delia did.

She was probably right this minute heading back toward the house, channeling her loss into that cool calm collected front she'd perfected.

She'd be hell to live with today, he knew. Not that he was a glutton for punishment, but he figured that being the bearer of bad news would not endear him to her. She'd probably go after his hide, rather than silently torture herself all day.

Who was he kidding? He wanted to find her, haul her close and never let go.

He clenched his hands into fists at his sides. The burning ache to hold her in his arms could not be endured. With a heartfelt oath, he left the barn to find her.

Only, she wasn't heading toward the house as he'd first assumed. No, somewhere along the way, his city girl must have lost a good part of her reserve about the wilderness, because she was heading toward the hills, her long legs striding with purposeful confidence, her shoulders back and proud.

She didn't want his company.

He followed, anyway.

* * *

Delia didn't know where she was headed, only that she had to go. Her vision wavered with each step she took, and her throat and chest burned so badly she could scarcely breathe.

But soon walking didn't satisfy her. It wasn't fast enough, wasn't taking her far enough, so she burst into a run and let loose through the woods as fast as she could go.

When she was beyond exhaustion, she stopped, sagging against a tree. Over the blood roaring in her ears, she could hear the river.

Staggering, she turned toward it and found herself on a high bank, staring down at the river as it rushed past rocks and sand. She stood there all alone with her misery, with God's glory spread out before her.

How had things fallen apart so, when only days ago she'd felt as though she had the world in her palm?

She wasn't heir.

She wasn't going to get Jacob.

Her heritage was one of greed and selfishness.

And the only man she might have ever been able to love didn't, or couldn't, love her back.

That last thought pretty much burst the fragile dam she'd been clinging to. With the tears finally overflowing, she sank to her knees on the frozen bank of the river and dropped her head into her hands.

* * *

Cade found her like that, kneeling away from him, sobbing her heart out in tune with the river. It was heart-wrenching, made all the more so because he knew she felt as if she had no choice but to hide to cry.

She truly believed she was completely alone in this.

"Delia."

She jerked, the only sign she'd heard him, and went utterly still. Her shoulders stiffened with the weight she carried, and in that moment he would have done anything to ease her burden.

How to make this better?

There was a gap between them, a gap he'd put there. What would happen if he breached it just this once?

"I'm sorry," he said quietly. "I'm so sorry."

She didn't move, just remained terribly silent.

"I know it didn't work out the way you wanted, but it can still—"

"Go away." She said this quite clearly, though her voice broke slightly on the last syllable. "Just leave me alone."

"Delia." Was he supposed to be able to do that? "You're crying, let me—"

"I'm not crying," she said fiercely, taking care to keep her back to him. Her long golden hair fell forward, exposing her sweet neck, making her look young, too young for all she'd been through, and so sad his heart ached. "I told you, I'm fine."

She was shaking with the effort to hold back the storm of tears he'd interrupted, he could see that now. And something within him trembled, too. "Delia, please." He sank to his knees behind her and put his hands on her shoulders, moving slowly, afraid to spook her; she felt as fragile as priceless china. He slid his hands down her arms to her hands and linked their fingers. He wanted to turn her around and hug her tight, but she had to do this, had to make the decision to let herself go in front of him. Gently he tugged at her resisting form, pulling her back against his chest. "Let me in. Come on, sweetheart, let me in."

"No." She held back, until their bodies touched, until he crossed their joined hands in front of her, hugging her tightly to him, bending over her shoulder to press his cheek to hers.

"No," she said again, less firmly and with far more tension in her husky voice.

"Yes," he whispered, rubbing his jaw on hers. "You're not alone in this. I'm right here and I'm not going anywhere."

"But for how long?" She struggled again. "Until your past haunts you again and you take off?"

No one knew better than he that truth hurts far more than lies. He closed his eyes, feeling the pain his actions had caused. "Never mind," she choked out, trying to free herself. "Just never mind. Go away, Cade."

As if he could. Holding her close, he put his

mouth to her ear. "I can't...I'm not going any-where."

"You will. You won't be able to help yourself."

"That's not why you were crying."

"I'm nothing more than a huge mistake." She tried to turn away from him, but he held on to her.

"Delia...no, not a mistake."

"Go away, Cade."

She needed tough love, he decided, and he was frustrated enough to give it to her. "So you're not Ethan's daughter, all the better since he was a jerk, anyway. Now you know for certain you don't share his blood."

That really stiffened her spine. "And I know for certain I'm not the heir."

"So you're not the heir. Don't you see? It doesn't matter. Maddie is the only one left, and she's always said if she turned out to be the one, she'd put Triple M in all three of your names."

Still angry and humiliated, Delia wouldn't look at him, but he could tell she was soaking up his words with a quivering intensity that broke his heart. He went on, "And yes, Scott is a sneaky jerk. And he might try to cause trouble, but he has his own weaknesses, and that gives us some le-verage. The judge can't ignore what we've told him. He can't overlook it." As Cade spoke, he stroked her back, trying to break through the wall she'd erected between them. "Are you listening, Delia? Do you understand? Scott can't hurt you."

"I understand, but really, I'm fine."

He swore, one particular vulgar oath that wasn't enough to express his frustration. ''Don't lie, not to me. You're not fine. You're just too damn stubborn to admit it.''

''My mother was stubborn,'' she said dully.

''How can you compare yourself to a woman who never deserved to have such a wonderful compassionate sensitive daughter?''

''It's true.''

''You're going to make me really mad, Delia.''

Her reaction surprised him. She let out a laugh. Then with a soft sob, she twisted in his arms and buried her face in his neck, plastering that long willowy body he'd been dreaming about to his.

Because she'd startled him, they fell to the frozen ground, and he stretched out, grabbing her and hugging her close. ''Let it go,'' he whispered, gently stroking her wildly trembling body. It was cold, they needed to get up, but she was going to shatter if she didn't let it go. ''Come on, baby.''

''I...can't.''

''I'm right here, you're not alone.''

''No, I...''

In spite of herself she burst into tears. Feeling helpless, he pulled her closer, murmuring wordlessly in her ear as she let go with a hard reluctance. She cried with such pent-up passion that he knew she'd stored this all up inside for far too long.

She wasn't a graceful crier, but messy and noisy, which was so inexplicably endearing he could hardly breathe. Finally she quieted, but still kept her face buried against him.

"All I've ever wanted is to help you, Delia. I...I have money. I've wanted to offer it to you several times, but I knew you'd never accept—"

"No," she said flatly, and lifted her head. "No."

"You know I was an attorney, before my wife and son... Before." He tucked a strand of wayward hair behind her ear. "I have a lot of money, more than I know what to do with. You can use it to—"

"No." She pushed away from him and lay flat on her back, looking up into the stark sky. "I won't be a user, like my parents were."

"It's not the same—"

"If I'm going to be their daughter, and it appears I have no choice, I sure won't be like them. It's enough that I have to live with the knowledge that all my life I've wanted nothing more than security. Maybe I didn't mean money, exactly, but it equaled the same thing, which makes me no better than they were."

"Accepting my help is not the same thing."

She sat, hugged her knees and looked so miserable he felt torn to shreds.

"I've never meant to hurt you," he said quietly. "Never."

"I know." Her eyes met his. "And I'm not that stubborn, Cade. If it comes right down to it, I'll ask for help before I lose Jacob."

"But you could have so much more…"

"No, I can't," she said softly. "I can't have the 'more' that I want."

"Delia." How to tell her he thought that maybe the "more" she wanted was exactly the same thing he wanted. But the thought was so unnerving he didn't know what to do with it. Instead, he reached over and pulled her close.

It started out as comforting. Warm. Safe. But then they shifted, and he felt her curves and soft skin. Her lips brushed his throat once, then his jaw, and the touch spread wildfire through his body. Before he could stop himself, he whispered her name in a voice thick and raspy with longing.

In response, she snuggled closer, and he wondered if she wanted more comfort or just…but then she slid her tongue over his skin, giving him his answer. When she did it again, he made a strangled sound that he couldn't control, and she froze.

"Is that…?" she began. "Was that wrong?"

Was she kidding? If it'd been any more right, he'd have died right there on the spot. With his fingers he pushed her hair away from her eyes and lifted her face.

"You can never go wrong when you touch me," he told her, watching her anxiety fade. "Ever."

She smiled, a curious combination of come-hither and innocence. "Maybe you're cold?" she asked.

"Not with your body pressed against me."

"Okay, good." Once again she buried her face

in his neck. "You always smell so good, good enough to…" She bit him lightly, then sucked that skin into her mouth.

Unsettled by how quickly his body went from the comforter to the seduced, he inhaled sharply. He was as aroused as he'd ever been, with just one touch of her tongue.

"Kiss me," she whispered. "Kiss me and make me forget." She didn't wait for him to comply, but reached up, threaded her fingers into his hair and pulled his mouth down to hers. "Don't make me beg."

"I'll be the one begging," he managed, trying his damnedest to remember how vulnerable she was right now, how he couldn't possibly take advantage. But then she touched the tip of her tongue to the corner of his mouth, her blue eyes clear now and very aware.

"Kiss me," she whispered again.

Helpless to resist, he did just that, pressing hard against her before he could think. Then there was no room to think because he had her warm lush body sprawled beneath him, her breasts plumped against his chest, her thighs spread to accommodate his. His hands slid down her sides, then back up, finding their way beneath her soft sweater, over her quivering stomach and ribs to cup her breasts.

"Yes," she gasped, arching into his palms, and he crushed her to him for more mind-blowing kisses, each beginning before the last one finished. It shouldn't have surprised him how right it felt to hold her, to touch her, to just be here with her. He'd been with other women since he was widowed, but always as a mutual physical release.

This wasn't just physical, and it sure as hell wasn't going to be something he could easily walk away from, but even that didn't stop him.

Nothing could have stopped him, except Delia herself.

His fingers found the thin straps of her bra, and he pulled them down. He slid up her sweater, baring her to his gaze, and when he looked down at her, saw her full curves, the dusky peaks hard and pebbled, he thought he'd never seen anything so beautiful. Hands suddenly unsteady, he held her still, bent his head and drew one of the pouty nipples into his mouth, sucking gently as she gasped his name and gripped him more tightly. Her hips were undulating in a rhythm against his, and when he stroked a hand down to them, seeking her heat, her center, he found her soaked from the ground.

They were lying on the ground, the frozen ground, which their bodies had heated up and thawed. "Delia…" She would catch a cold.

Hell, he would catch a cold, too, given the way she had him puffing air as if he'd run a five-mile race uphill. But she didn't seem to care, if the throaty little pants she was letting out were any indication. And because he was powerless to resist, he rasped a thumb over her nipple one last time. "Honey…"

She tossed back her head, eyes closed as if she'd

never experienced anything like this before, and yet she boldly slid her hands down the back of him, cupping his buttocks, bringing him closer to the heaven between her thighs. He groaned as his raging erection slid over her moist heat, his vision nothing but a haze now. "We have to stop. Delia, we can't...not here."

Her eyes opened, her gaze unfocused and sexy as hell. "What?" Her voice was low.

"We have to get up."

Slowly, she blinked him into focus, her eyelashes still damp from her crying jag. "Stop?"

It was the last thing he wanted to do. "Yeah."

"I see." She pushed free and straightened her clothing—which meant she hid the most incredible body he'd ever seen from him—and shoved her hair out of her face. She stood, weaving a bit, until he stood, also, and steadied her. "I said I'm okay." She took a step back from his assisting hands.

"Delia." Gently he rubbed at the tracks of tears on her soft cheeks. "Don't vanish behind that cool calm of yours. Please don't. You don't have to always be the strong one."

Her look told him she didn't believe that. Her words told him even more. "The case is over for you. Maddie's the heir by default, which means you're free to leave. That must feel...well, freeing."

He stared at her, stunned. It was true he was free. It'd been what he'd wanted, what he'd craved, and he hadn't even realized it was now his for the taking.

"Oh, my God," she whispered. "That didn't occur to you until just now, that you're able to leave here, forever. I don't know if that makes me feel better or worse."

She looked away from him, self-consciously tugging at her sweater, which revealed her still-hard nipples. "You were right." Tipping back her head, she stared up into the sky. "I've held back from the people I care about most, and that's unforgivable. I need to fix that."

Then with one last long inscrutable look into his eyes, she turned and started walking away.

"Wait! Where are you going?"

"To tell my sisters the truth," she said over her shoulder. "I'm going to tell them everything." Then she disappeared into the woods, heading toward the house.

Well, he'd walked right into that one. She considered her sisters the most important people in her life. Not him. She wouldn't think that way about him, not when he'd done his best to hold back from her, as well. But dammit, couldn't he have also been included in that group?

Cade sank back onto the ground, heedless of the cold, his heart racing, pulse drumming, as he realized the sorry truth. He hadn't protected or withheld his heart at all.

He'd fallen in love with her.

* * *

Delia marched into the house, prepared to drop the weight of her past and Maddie's future as the heir off her shoulders, so when she found herself alone, her shoulders sagged in disappointment.

Where were they?

Then she heard voices coming from their office. The wedding, she figured. With only days left, they'd be discussing flowers, food and fun, the three required *F*'s for a wedding.

"We can give him the first room on the left," came Maddie's excited voice. "So he's close to all the action. He'll want that. Any eight-year-old would."

Jacob, Delia realized with surprise. They were talking about Jacob.

"You can't give a boy that option," Zoe answered, disagreeing mildly. "Granted, he looks sweet enough, but he is a boy, and therefore trouble with a capital *T*. He'll need far more supervision than that. Trust me on this, I know such things, being a fellow wild one. I think he should be near me—"

Maddie laughed. "I see right through you, Zoe Martin. You want him for yourself. And you pretend to be so tough."

"I *am* tough."

"I can't wait," Maddie said dreamily. "A little boy. Can you imagine how different his life will be here? How much better off…"

The voices didn't fade as Delia moved closer to the office, but the meaning of the words escaped her as she realized it was no one's fault but her own if they got hurt. She had to tell them the truth.

But where to start?

She knew how much Zoe had once wanted to be the heir. She knew exactly how badly she herself had wanted to be heir. But she had no idea about Maddie, who'd been strangely closed-mouthed about the whole thing.

Well, she'd just start at the beginning and hope she could get it all out without hurting her sisters any more than she already had.

"Jacob might not be coming," Delia said quietly after opening the door and facing both her startled sisters. "I've lied to both of you." She drew on her last reserves of strength, knowing she had Cade to thank for having any left at all. "The truth is, I was told months ago by the social worker on Jacob's case I wasn't worth enough to get Jacob—"

"What?" Shock filled Maddie's gaze. "You were told what? And by whom? How dare they! Your heart alone is worth its weight in gold—how could they not know that? I want a name, dammit, and I want a number, too! Just wait until I get hold of those people."

Maddie never swore. Delia stared at her. "His name is Scott Felton, and Maddie, murder is a capital offense."

Zoe gave a tight smile. "Only if you're caught. What do they mean, you're not worth enough, Delia?"

"Exactly what it sounds like." Weary, Delia sank into a chair. "Jacob comes with that large inheritance from his father, which can't just go to anyone. It has to be managed. Edna is wealthy in her own right and can easily manage a sum like that."

"But you're his sister," Zoe pointed out. "That counts for more than wealth. Besides, you have this place."

"Which, until we actually make money, isn't worth much. And actually, no, I don't have it."

"Well, maybe not technically," Zoe said, waving that off. "Not until Cade proves who's really the heir, but what the heck does that matter? One of the three of us own it, and that's good enough."

For the second time in as many hours, Delia came close to breaking. Their love never failed to blow her away. "It's not good enough for the courts," she said.

"Well, it should be," Maddie fumed. "But since it's not, take it. Let's put your name on the deed." She looked at Zoe, who nodded without hesitation.

"Absolutely," Zoe agreed. "Let's do it. Call Cade in here, he can—"

"No." Delia drew a deep ragged breath. "I can't let you do that."

"Try and stop me," Maddie said firmly, then softened. "Oh, honey, how could you not tell us?"

"I'm sorry," Delia whispered, closing her eyes in misery. "It seems so dumb now."

"Sure does," Zoe said. "Now let's get Cade."

"I...I was just with him." Two avidly curious gazes ran over her, suddenly taking in the wild state of her hair, her damp clothing and the rosiness she still felt in her cheeks from Cade's kisses deepening into a full-blown blush. "I mean, we were just talking..."

Zoe crossed her arms, a wide grin on her face. "Uh-huh. Just talking. That's why your hair is a mess—with a stick in it, I see. And you have mud all over your butt, Dee. And you call that talking, too?"

Maddie's eyebrows shot up as she looked Delia over. "You do have a sort of ravished look about you, honey. Did you—"

"No," Delia said quickly. "We didn't. And we did talk. I'm not ever going to be heir—it's just not possible. My father was really a man named Eddie Kitze, not Ethan Constance. Which means—" she took Maddie's hand and managed to smile into her questioning eyes "—you must be the heir."

Maddie blinked slowly. *"What?"*

"You're the heir, Maddie. And I don't think it could have happened to a more deserving woman."

Maddie continued to stand there, looking shell-shocked.

Zoe hugged Maddie, her eyes glued to Delia over Maddie's head.

Maddie looked at Delia too. "I don't want to be the heir. I want *you* to be the heir."

"Maddie—"

"No, you listen to me, Delia." Maddie's eyes flashed with temper. "You've been keeping secrets, not out of meanness, but from some misguided notion you have to keep all your problems to yourself. As if you couldn't trust us with your heart. *Us!* You lied, and while I know you didn't mean to hurt us, you did."

Delia couldn't have felt more like slime. "God, Maddie…"

"I don't want to be the heir," she whispered, sinking into a chair next to Delia. "I want Delia to be the heir. I want Jacob here with us, where he belongs. I want…" She let out a little laugh. "I want everything."

Zoe dropped to her knees in front of her sisters, and the three of them held one another. "I want everything, too," Zoe said. "And since we deserve it, dammit, let's just get it, okay? We'll put Delia's name on the deed for now, we'll take the judge by storm, and we'll…"

"You forgive me," Delia said, overwhelmed with awe and love. She chuckled when Zoe smacked her lightly, then hugged her tight.

"You idiot," both Maddie and Zoe said at the same time, then they all laughed through their tears because nothing between them would ever change.

They forgave her. Delia couldn't get over it, steeped as she was in their love.

Only months ago, her life would have been complete with just the knowledge that they would never turn her away. But now she thought of Cade and what could never be, and she sighed deeply, holding on tight to the most wonderful sisters anyone could ask for.

And wanting still more.

Chapter 13

Zoe and Ty's wedding day arrived, sunny and breezy and glorious. To everyone's joy, Edna flew in with Jacob.

With the custody hearing only days away, Delia thought she'd be a nervous wreck, but having Jacob close by settled her nerves as nothing else could have.

She stood near the altar with Maddie, both of them dressed in the midnight-blue silky dresses she'd made, waiting for Zoe to walk down the aisle of the small church.

Across from her stood Ty, tall, dark and gorgeous, staring intently at the door at the end of the aisle. He was waiting with barely restrained patience for a glimpse of his bride.

Next to Ty stood Cade, the best man, also tall, dark and gorgeous. And staring.

At her.

She lifted a brow, questioning, but he didn't move, just kept looking at her, and it was such a deeply personal questing stare she could do nothing but return it. She felt as though she could see so much in his eyes—hope and happiness and passion. And strength—strength he'd share with her whenever her own faltered.

Yet he was leaving; he had to be. He was done with the case and she knew he wouldn't, couldn't, ever be happy in one spot.

Zoe appeared then, and Delia's attention was momentarily diverted. Yet, beautiful as her sister looked in the gown she'd created, as wonderful and touching as the ceremony was, Delia couldn't get her mind off Cade. The way he was watching her, warming her with his sensual knowing gaze.

What was he thinking as he looked at her like that, as if she was the only woman in the world?

Ty and Zoe held hands as they spoke their vows, their gazes filled with such wonder and love that Delia had to look away, or the deep ache inside her might consume her.

She didn't want Cade to go, maybe she'd *never* wanted him to go.

He was intelligent, funny, passionate, and the most caring man she'd ever met. He was on her mind from the moment she awoke in the morning until she fell asleep at night. She dreamed about him and got up with the memory of his taste, his touch, and instead of being satisfied, she wanted more. She wanted all of him, and it wasn't just a physical wanting, though her body yearned and burned.

With all her heart she wanted him to stay.

Forever.

The thought made her gasp out loud, and Maddie shot her a surprised look, but Delia regained her composure quickly, for it was foolish to wonder what it would be like to have Cade forever.

Ty leaned close to Zoe and kissed her hard and long. Cade and Maddie laughed and clapped, Edna looked touched, and as the kiss dragged on, Jacob wore an expression between feigned disgust and happiness. Delia smiled, but she couldn't tear her gaze away from Cade.

Later, after everyone had left the church and they were at dinner together, Cade pulled Delia aside and gazed deeply into her eyes. "Do you have any idea how beautiful you are?"

His words stole her breath. "You've seen beautiful women before."

Not denying that, he laughed softly, sexily, and blocking her from the others with his body, he stroked a work-roughened thumb over her jaw. "What's on that gorgeous mind of yours, Delia? It's not another woman."

"Yes. Yes, it is," she whispered. "I want to know about your wife."

His thumb stilled. "I'm not comparing the two of you, if that's what you're thinking."

"Because there's no comparison?"

"Because you're so different." He sighed when she only waited for more. "I loved Lisa. We were high-school sweethearts. Best friends. We were...comfortable. Cozy." His gaze waited for hers. "What you and I have, Delia, has never been cozy."

"No. Not cozy."

His eyes heated and he touched her again, making her shiver.

"Would you ever be happy staying here?" Shocked and horrified at herself, she scrambled to backpedal. "Never mind. Just...never mind." When she tried to step away, he stopped her.

"I didn't know you thought of me like that," he said, clearly surprised.

"Yeah, well, don't let it go to your head." Determined to let nothing ruin this day, Zoe's wedding day, she again tried to turn away.

And again he stopped her. "Just because I've avoided commitment since my family's death doesn't mean I don't know the meaning of the word," he murmured, watching his fingers on her arm as he ran them down to her fingers to link their hands. Then he raised their joined hands to his lips. "I don't know what to do about you, Delia. God help me, I just don't."

What did that mean? Whatever it meant, he wasn't offering undying love, that was certain. And anyway, she didn't need it. She had everything that mattered. Her life was perfect as it was, or it would be after the custody hearing.

She tried to pull away once more, afraid to let him see into her eyes, because all she felt for him was there, leaving her far more vulnerable than she'd ever been in her life.

"Delia—"

"No, don't." And with a tug, she broke free.

Jacob was at the table when she got there, watching her carefully, and she smiled at him.

"You look funny," he said, his brow puckering. "You're not going to…cry or anything, are you?"

"No." Swallowing hard, she forced another smile.

The fact that Cade was indeed the prince she'd been looking for all her life didn't escape her and certainly didn't help her already-bruised pride.

She didn't want to need him as much as she did, didn't want to need anyone.

The restaurant had a small dance floor and a three-piece band. But they were good, and it wasn't long before Ty dragged Zoe out onto the floor for a dance.

Cade watched them for a moment, locked in each other's arms and apparently lost in each other. The way Ty held Zoe, the way she looked at him, stirred the emptiness in his own heart.

Automatically, without even realizing what he was doing, he searched out Delia. And found her, quietly watching him. The now familiar confusion hit him, the one that always came when he looked at her.

Her light eyes were clear and warm. The soft flickering glow of the candles gave her skin a pearly luster. Her glorious hair, loose and wavy to her shoulders, shone.

Delia by candlelight.

He'd never seen anyone lovelier.

Slowly, almost against his will, he moved toward her. Her eyes widened when his intent became clear, but his Delia, his strong valiant steady Delia, held her ground.

"Come with me," he said, taking her hand and pulling her up.

"What are you doing?" she asked in an alarmed whisper, glancing back at Maddie, who just smiled serenely.

Cade smiled, too, and didn't let go of her, so that short of making a scene, she had little to no choice other than to follow him. She managed to throw a smile back to Maddie and the others, but he could feel how stiff she was.

"Relax," he murmured in her ear, drawing her close for a slow dance he knew would be pure torture.

"I can't!"

"Sure you can. You just take a deep breath and—"

"No, dammit! I mean, I can't dance!"

He laughed, but when she went even stiffer, he

eased back and looked at her. "You're not kidding?" For some ridiculous reason tenderness filled him. It meant that no one had ever held her quite like this, which shouldn't have been so thrilling. The music obliged him, became slower more sensual, and there in the dark they began to move to the beat.

"I don't know what to do," she whispered, clearly flustered. "Or where to put my hands…or my feet."

"Just ease up against me…yeah, that's it. Put your hands here…" He wrapped one around his neck. "And here…" He entwined her fingers with his, drawing her against him. Ignoring the shaft of heat that caused, he smiled into her tense face. "This is supposed to be fun, you know."

"Fun," she muttered, but she swayed with him, holding him as if she liked it in spite of herself. "We're awfully close."

"That's the idea." He held her gaze as she blushed. Then she tucked her face into the crook of his neck, which was just as good because now he could feel her every little breath, which seemed to be coming faster and faster.

Cade could have drowned in the pleasure of it.

We're awfully close.

It'd been a problem for both of them since the first time they'd met. But he found that he no longer had the will to fight that closeness, that he actually wanted to savor it, go with it. For him, it was like coming out of a dark tunnel, one he'd been in for eight long years. It was like feeling the warmth of the sun on his face after a cold and bitter winter.

His body gravitated toward hers until there wasn't an inch of space between them as they moved to the music. Her fingers were curled in the ends of his hair, stroking lightly in a caress he wasn't sure she was even aware of; but he was, so much so that he had to close his eyes. But all that did was intensify everything. The feel of her soft body against his firm one, the easy flow of her movements, the heat those movements generated.

When he rocked, she rocked, and she let out a little sigh, losing the last of her resistance. He nearly groaned out loud. Her touch felt good, too good, and the feel of her arms around him only added to the sweet pain. He buried his face in her hair and held on tight, wondering if she could feel his heart racing, wondering if she knew he was as hard as a rock.

Just then she looked up at him, her gaze filled with wonder, and an awareness that made him catch his breath.

She knew.

Slowly she slid her hips over his. His arousal throbbed.

"Delia."

In answer, she did it again.

Oh, yeah, she'd definitely noticed.

"I think I've got the hang of this slow-dancing

thing,'' she whispered, drawing back as the music ended. ''What do you think?''

He thought she was part witch, part angel. He thought he might haul her off and have his merry way with her in the parking lot. He thought... Oh, hell. He thought he was in love with her. In love with a woman afraid of the word. ''I think... I *know* I want you. Delia, I want you more than I want my next breath.''

''I want you, too, but—''

''The but,'' he muttered. ''There's always a but.''

''Sometimes there has to be.''

''I don't know why.''

''Because this is complicated.''

''There's another word I don't like.''

Her expression saddened. ''I'm not capable of uncomplicated unattached sex,'' she said, and while he wanted to laugh, he couldn't.

He knew Delia would never give herself without love. But *could* she love? ''What if it's not just sex?'' he asked.

''It's not anything more,'' she said quickly. ''It can't be.''

''Why?''

''Why?'' She let out a small laugh that didn't fool either of them. ''What a silly question.''

''Not silly. Answer it.''

''Okay,'' she said slowly, obviously scrambling for thoughts. ''It's not more because...because I have too much going on, that's why. I have my sisters, the ranch, Jacob—''

"Excuses." Gently he cupped her face. "All excuses."

"The truth," she said firmly, but her rapidly rising and falling chest told him the real truth.

She was afraid. He knew that, just as he knew
he wasn't ready to admit his own feelings to her.

Didn't know if he ever would be.

Jacob called her just then, and Zoe was about to
toss her bouquet, and for the rest of the evening,
Delia made sure she was too busy to give Cade
more than a glance, though glance she did, and
often, in a way that made it clear to him she was
unsettled and off balance.

Well, good, he thought grimly.

That made two of them.

Delia knew that Cade hoped she would go to his
room that night. She also knew that making love
with him would be the most sensual erotic experience of her inexperienced life. He was amazingly
in tune to her, and so damn sexy her knees went
weak if he merely smiled.

He'd opened his wounds for her, had made himself vulnerable. She knew he expected the same of
her.

She couldn't do it. She'd never done it, bared
her heart and soul completely, other than that time
out by the river where she'd sobbed in his arms.
Just thinking about it brought a flush to her face.
Of course when she remembered what followed, of
how he'd touched and kissed her as though she was
the most precious woman on earth, that flush of

shame turned into something else entirely. Her entire body tingled at the memory.

Now, without further thought, she might have gone to Cade, might have followed her body's cravings, if it hadn't been for the phone call.

It was Scott.

"I'd like to see you before the judge's ruling," he said. He sounded surprisingly open and friendly.

She was alone in the office. Zoe and Ty had stayed in Rawlings for their wedding night. Maddie, Edna and Jacob had already gone to bed, and Cade... She had no idea where Cade had gone, only knew that she wasn't going to easily fall asleep when she remembered that last hungry all-consuming look he'd given her.

Now Scott was on the phone, as pleasant as if they'd never had any harsh words between them. "I don't know if that's a good idea," she said.

"Please?" His voice softened even more. "I haven't been as honest as I could, and I know that. I think we can work this out..."

While she knew Scott hadn't faced any job repercussions—yet—she had hopes that he would. Did Scott know they'd sent the judge a letter outlining their concerns about him as Jacob's social worker?

No, he didn't know, she decided, or he never would have bothered to call her now. "Are you withdrawing your request for custody?"

"I know how much Jacob means to you," he said. "I've seen you with him."

''He's my family. So have you, Scott? Have you withdrawn your request?''

''You know, this is too important to discuss over the telephone.''

He was right about that much.

''We're meeting the judge in two days,'' he said urgently. ''All I'm asking is that you come in one day early and meet with me. It's your brother's future, and yours. But if I'm asking too much…?''

''No,'' she said. ''Of course not.''

They agreed on a restaurant to meet the night before the judge's ruling, which meant tomorrow night.

So close, and yet an eternity away.

For a long time after she hung up, Delia sat there alone in the dark office. She didn't have to be alone. She could seek out Cade, open her heart and spill her worries. He'd welcome her.

She could tell him everything, then ask him to come with her to L.A., and he would, she knew, without hesitation.

But her old fierce independence reared its head. She had to remind herself she didn't need him, though that was getting more and more difficult. In fact, it was almost a pretense now, because the truth was she *did* need him. Too much for her own comfort.

She'd deal with that after Jacob, she promised herself. One way or another.

Chapter 14

Cade couldn't believe it when he finally got Zoe to admit that Delia had left for Los Angeles to meet Scott. Alone.

He'd thought they'd made strides in the trust department, but apparently he'd been wrong. She didn't trust him, she didn't need him. Didn't that just about sum up the sorry existence he'd been living? He didn't want to trust, either, and sure as hell didn't want to need, but he did.

And though he hadn't imagined himself ready to say these things to a woman ever again, he thought maybe he was ready to say them now.

To Delia.

Only she didn't want to hear them.

Dammit, he'd blown everything. He should have

told her sooner. He thought of little else on the long flight to California.

When he finally caught up with her in the restaurant Zoe had named, sitting opposite Scott at a cozy little table as if they were fast friends, he had trouble keeping calm. Until he got closer and had a good look at them.

Scott was grim-faced, Delia pale as a ghost.

Uninvited, Cade grabbed a chair and sat at their table, without a thought to sensibilities and politeness. Never taking his eyes off Delia, he leaned forward and put her icy hand in his. "Hey."

Delia blinked him into focus and made a startled sound before surging to her feet.

Standing, too, Cade reached for her shoulders, concerned at the way she was shaking. "Delia? Talk to me."

"Not here," she said, closing her eyes briefly, then leveling them on Cade in that deliberately cool steady gaze he now knew meant she was struggling for control. "We're out of here."

Her hand still on his, which gave him a tiny bit of comfort, she started to make her way to the door.

Scott called after her and she paused.

"What are you going to do?" he wanted to know.

A look of fear and something deeper and darker flickered across her face, but then was gone. Delia lifted her chin. "I'm going to win without playing dirty,'' she said, and then kept walking, head high, hips swaying gently.

A haze of red fury settled across Cade's vision. He wanted to demand answers, wanted to pound Scott for putting that look in her eyes, but he had a feeling Delia wouldn't appreciate any caveman techniques.

So he went with her silently, seething for her, at her, until they were standing on the sidewalk in the uncomfortably warm Los Angeles night.

Delia fumbled through her purse. ''My keys,'' she muttered. ''They're…here.'' Then calmly, she unlocked her rental car, and Cade might have thought she'd already forgotten Scott except for the tremor in her hands.

''Delia.'' He took the keys from her shaking fingers. ''Talk to me.''

''I'm fine.'' But she stared down at the opened car door as if she'd forgotten what she was doing. ''I'm just fine.''

''Is that how you want to play this? As if you're superwoman?''

''For now,'' she mumbled, but when he reached for her, she clutched his shirtfront and held on tight. ''I…I want to go to my hotel. Now.''

''Good. Let's go.''

''You're coming with me?''

She seemed shocked, and embarrassed, too, as if she knew he was good and angry. ''I'd go with you to the ends of the earth,'' he said quite seriously, ''if you asked.''

She looked as if she was going to cry, which was the last thing he'd intended. "Get in," he said, gently pushing her into the car. "Move over."

"But what about your car? And how did you find—" She squeaked when he nearly sat on her and she hastily scooted over.

"The hotel," he said firmly. "We'll play twenty questions there, but you're going first." He slammed the car into gear. "And, Delia? I'm going to want to hear every bit of it. No half-truths, no holding back. I want it all."

She blinked at him slowly, then gave him a watery smile. "It's okay," she said. "I'm done being a coward."

What did that mean? But before he could ask, she set her hand on his thigh, leaned in close and kissed him softly on the cheek. "Thank you," she whispered.

The touch of her lips on his skin had him almost quivering like a pathetic puppy, which annoyed the hell out of him. He wanted his anger back—it was much easier to handle. "What was that for?"

"For caring for me." Her gaze was rueful. "I haven't made it easy, have I?"

He had to smile at that as he pulled the car out of the lot. "Delia, easy is just about the last thing I'd call you."

She'd already checked into the hotel, so they went directly up to her room.

By the time they got there, Delia's heart was

threatening to bounce right out of her chest. She'd been alone, handling Scott, doing just fine despite his attempt to blackmail her with an episode from her past she'd rather forget, when Cade had walked in.

Clearly furious, edgy and just a bit dangerous-looking, he'd made her heart soar. Never in her life had she been so glad to see someone, and that it was Cade who made her feel that way no longer shocked her.

Right then and there, in the middle of an emotional battle for her brother, for her future, for everything, the truth had come to her. She was indeed a coward. She'd actually become more terrified of Cade's smile than of the outcome of the custody battle.

How sad was that?

Especially when the truth was, being with Cade, talking with him, laughing with him, just existing with him, made her feel whole.

It was time, past time, to get over her fear of letting Cade really know her. It was time to get over her virginity, too, she decided. Maybe then she wouldn't be so…uptight. She had no idea what would come of it, but she was tired of feeling so wound up, so vibrantly aware of the tall, dark and brooding man behind her.

Why hadn't she seen it sooner? Making love with him would help. It would *have* to help.

He opened the door, his eyes on her, deep and full of things that made her heat up from the inside

out. He was still angry. He was most definitely full
of questions. And so taut with tension every muscle she could see was delineated.

Did he still want her? She hoped so. She wanted
him.

Right now, as a matter of fact.

They entered the room in silence, Delia's
thoughts racing as she planned her seduction. Cade
was quiet, too quiet.

Until she shut the door.

Tossing his jacket on the bed, he turned toward
her, his hands fisted on his hips, his shoulders tight,
mouth grim. "Did he threaten you? Hurt you in
any way?"

Because her thoughts had been running in an
entirely different direction—did he have any idea
how sexy he looked?—she had a hard time keeping
up with him. "What?"

With an oath, he crossed to her, grasped her
arms and hauled her close. "Dammit, you're driving me crazy! How could you still shut me out,
after all this time? You still won't let me in your
head. When I figured out what you'd planned, I
nearly had a heart attack." He drew in a shuddery
breath, then let it out slowly. "Never mind. I'm
sorry, it doesn't matter now. None of it does. Just
tell me…are you okay?" He held her slightly away
from him.

"Yes, I'm…quite fine." Breathless and
strangely achy, maybe. Definitely nervous, but
first-time jitters were to be expected, right?

''Tell me everything.''

''Okay. On the phone, Scott said he wanted to meet with me and apologize, but that was a lie. He had me investigated and…found something he can use against me if I don't withdraw my custody request.''

''What?''

Delia stepped farther away and turned her back to him, wishing she didn't have to say it. ''I shoplifted once.'' She stared hard out the window. ''I was arrested. It's on my juvenile record, which is sealed, so I'm not sure how—''

''Oh, Delia,'' he breathed softly. ''How did—''

''I was fifteen,'' she said, ''and Maddie had gotten herself restricted. She'd missed dinner, then overslept breakfast, and on the way to school, she nearly passed out. We didn't have any money, and there was the doughnut shop, so…'' She shrugged as if it didn't matter, but it did. Still did. She'd never forget the owner's anger, how he'd insisted on filing charges for one lousy doughnut, how roughly she'd been treated at the police station, even though she was a minor on a first offense. She'd been terrified, and even now, the memory made her cringe.

''No, no, sweetheart. I meant, how did Scott find out?'' She felt his hands settle on her shoulders again and glide up and down her arms in a motion that was unbelievably comforting.

Too comforting. She stepped away. ''I don't know.''

"The point is, he's threatened you, and we're going to tell the judge. No one is going to hold your actions as a teenager against you. Delia, you were trying to feed your sister, for God's sake. No judge is going to consider you a criminal when he hears the story." His voice sounded tight, full of carefully restrained emotion, and she knew it was for her.

It was such a small thing, really, but to Delia, it felt like the world. He cared for her, and though she'd realized it before, it was as though it finally sank all the way in.

"Why did you go to see him alone?" When she didn't answer, he turned her back around to face him. "Why, Delia?"

"I'm sorry," she whispered, shaking her head. "I wish I hadn't. The moment I saw you, I was so relieved. I knew you'd help."

"Always."

"I wanted to take care of it myself, but the minute I sat down at the table and saw him, I knew I was wrong. I should have asked you to come."

The tension drained from his shoulders, and his eyes softened. "That asking part, it's so hard for you. I wish it wasn't."

"It's getting a bit easier." Now she wanted his hands back on her, on all of her, so she closed the distance between them, and slid her hands up his chest. "I need your help now, Cade."

"I know. We'll call the judge first thing in the morning, before the ruling. We'll—"

"That's not what I meant." She lifted her lashes and looked at him with all her yearning. She wasn't sure she had the look right. She'd never seduced a man before, but given the way his eyes widened, the way his mouth opened as if he had to do that simply to breathe, she thought maybe she'd come close. To be sure, she moved nearer, brushing her hips against his.

A groan escaped him and he tried to pull back. "Delia…" he said unsteadily.

"Make love with me, Cade."

He stared at her as if his mind had gone completely blank. Another sound escaped him, darker, thrilling.

"Is that a yes or no?" she asked, as if her heart wasn't in her throat, as if her body wasn't tingling in anticipation.

He framed her face with his hands, his mouth close enough to kiss hers, but he didn't. Instead, he searched her gaze. "What's going on, Delia?"

It annoyed her that desire had sharp claws, and that they were still digging into her so that she felt raw with this need for him, especially when he obviously didn't feel the same need for her. "What's going on is, I was obviously mistaken about your wanting me."

"You weren't wrong," he said roughly, even as his fingers drew soft little circles on her skin. "I want you so much I can't even think straight. But…why? Why now?"

"I've always wanted you. I was afraid, though."

"Of me?"

He looked so horrified, she had to smile. "Of *me*. Of how you make me feel. Jittery. Hot. Cold. Kiss me, Cade."

"Kiss me back," he whispered, and brought his mouth down on hers.

It was perfect. She poured everything she had into the kiss, all the longing, all the pent-up regret, all her...yes, dammit, all her love. She loved him, and the knowledge made her tremble.

He pulled back, skimmed his fingertips over her jaw. "You're shaking. I don't think—"

"Good. Don't think," she said, pulling him back down for another kiss. How to keep his attention? she wondered frantically. She knew the technicality of the whole thing, of this whole seduction, but she wasn't sure how to actually accomplish it. In her dreams, it hadn't seemed so difficult. She closed her eyes, drew a deep breath, stepped back and pulled her sweater over her head, which left her standing there in her pastel-yellow bra. Without waiting to see his reaction, she quickly pulled his head down to hers again and kissed him with far more eagerness than finesse.

For one eternally long moment, he hesitated, then with a small moan, pulled her close and kissed her once, then again from a different angle, then another, while he ran his hands down her back to her bottom and buried his face in her hair.

"What's under the skirt?" he asked hoarsely.

"Just...panties."

With characteristic boldness, he slid his hands down the backs of her legs, then up beneath the skirt, making her gasp.

"Stop?" he asked.

"No. Don't stop."

He shifted, his hands sliding up her ribs to capture her breasts, gliding over the bra, then opening the front clasp to expose her completely. Breathing hard, he drew back to look at her, his half-closed eyes glittering with passion. Her denim skirt had buttons down the front, and slowly, one by one, his sure fingers dispensed with them, until the material fell away. "Delia." His voice sounded awed, rough. "You're so beautiful."

"Now you," she murmured, pulling his shirt over his head, revealing tough sinew and rugged strength. She set her hands on his chest, sliding them back and forth over his hot skin, marveling at his body. Her insides were quivering. So were her knees, and she clutched at him until he scooped her up and lay her on the bed. His hands went to his pants as he stared down at her. When he shoved them down, she caught her breath, because *he* was the beautiful one, all molded and sculpted, and hard, very very hard.

He took out a condom and put it on while she watched with utter fascination. Then he was crawling onto the bed and covering her body with his, and thinking became next to impossible.

More so when he ran his hands over her, almost reverently, missing nothing, not her breasts, her stomach or the throbbing aching flesh between her legs. "This isn't a dream, right?" he whispered, his voice harsh with need. "I'm not going to wake up and find you gone, am I?"

Apparently he didn't require an answer because in the next split second, his mouth took hers. Over and over again his tongue and lips teased and tempted, while those clever hands stroked and tormented. "So sweet," he murmured, dipping to taste the hollow of her throat, the sensitive skin of her neck, the line of her collarbone. His touch had her writhing helplessly, seized with an unbearable tension. Swept along on the tide of pleasure, riding the wave of madness that had seized her body, she could do little more than strain toward him, letting out little panting whimpers.

"That's it," he whispered against her skin. "Come for me."

She couldn't have held back if she'd wanted, and arching against the bed, she exploded, shuddering endlessly, gasping for breath. When she could see and hear again, she lay there, staring up at the ceiling. "Holy cow."

His laugh was low and sexy. And strained, which made her lift her head and look at him. His eyes were fierce as he rose above her, braced himself and entered her.

Or tried to. At her tightness, he frowned, then pulled back a little and thrust again gently. The sensation of him starting to fill her was the most incredible thing she'd ever felt, and though he was barely inside her, she felt her body start to quiver again. "More," she cried, clutching at him, arching her hips to give him better access.

"I'm trying, but..." Something continued to block him, and he started to withdraw. At the threatened loss of his delicious weight, which was snatching back the promise of another explosive orgasm, Delia snagged his hips in her hands and yanked him toward her, which caused him to sink fully within her.

"There," she breathed. "Oh...there..."

Cade's heart nearly burst.

Her first. He was her first lover. He was all the way inside her now. Home. At the realization, his control broke instantly, and with a strangled groan, he gathered her hair in his fists, tipped her face up so he could meet her gaze and then thrust into her again, alive for the first time in eight years.

One stroke and he nearly came. Two strokes and she did, again, which triggered his own, an endless ripple of searing hot pleasure. Finally, finally, it eased, and he sank to his side, bringing her with him.

He had questions, a million of them, but primarily how could she have reached the age of twenty-six, looking as she did, and still be a virgin? But exhaustion claimed him, as it already had her, and holding her close in his arms, he let his eyes drift shut.

In the moment before he fell asleep, it came to him.

She'd never trusted a man before. Until him. His heart ached at that thought, but though he'd taken her virginity, he knew that the battle for her heart wasn't over yet.

Chapter 15

The courthouse was a beautiful brick-and-glass building, surrounded by lush greenery. An oasis in the middle of a teeming bustling city, but Delia saw none of it.

Her palms were damp, and her heart thudded dully in anticipation. Even with Cade's hand locked securely in hers, she could hardly remember how to walk. "What if—"

"You'll get him," Cade said, his voice still husky from sleep.

Just listening to it made Delia want to blush. She'd never felt like this, all hot and itchy and unsettled, and even more unnerving was the knowledge that it wasn't an entirely bad feeling.

They'd turned to each other several more times

in the night. Their lovemaking had been slow and tender, yet just as hot as the first time, and when they'd finally fallen into a deep slumber, they'd nearly missed the alarm.

Despite their lack of time, Cade had tried to talk about what had happened between them, and ashamed as Delia was to admit it, she'd put him off.

Yes, she'd been a virgin, and no, she had no regrets. How could she regret the most amazing night she'd ever spent?

Yes, she'd shattered in his arms as if she'd known what she was doing, but the why of it was still a mystery.

Which brought her to the last question she knew he wanted answered. Where were they going from here?

She hadn't a clue. What did she do with a man who didn't know how to stay in one spot?

No, that wasn't fair, because the truth was, it was *her* holding them back. Not him.

Shortly before they'd left the hotel, Cade tried again to get her to talk to him. He'd caught her in the bathroom and pressed his big body against hers. "Don't," he said, putting his hot wet open mouth to her neck.

"Don't what?" she said on a heartfelt moan.

"Shut me out. You're doing it, giving me the morning-after blow-off."

"I'm not…" But that was exactly what she was doing. "Cade, I don't…" She didn't what? Know how she felt? But that was a lie, she knew. She was just afraid of it. "We have to go," she had finally said, and when he went very still, then slowly drew back to look at her with an intensity that made her squirm, she sighed. "We really do have to go."

Without a further word, he'd left the bathroom, and they hadn't spoken as they'd raced out of the hotel to the courthouse.

As a result, Delia felt uncharacteristically ruffled. Because she couldn't breathe, she hesitated on the steps of the building and put a hand to her chest.

"You'll get him," Cade said again.

Even now he was offering his strength and comfort. She didn't deserve him, but she squeezed his hand and thanked him with her eyes.

The judge came in, sat down and didn't waste any time. He'd read the reports and the recommendations, he said, and was unhappy because he hated to see Jacob uprooted yet again. The boy was too young to have had such upheaval in his life. The judge then wanted to hear from the parties involved, wanted to be convinced this was the right thing to do. Then, leaning forward, looking kind but terribly stern, he waited expectantly.

Edna stood. "I love Jacob," she told him in her clear refined voice. "I can and will care for him for as long as I'm able, but I believe that he belongs with his sister. With Delia."

"In Idaho?" The judge lifted a questioning brow. "A thousand miles from his home?"

"Yes, Your Honor. I believe this is the right thing for Jacob, and that's all that matters to me. Doing right for him."

Heart thundering, Delia rose, also. "Your Honor, Jacob has been moved many times in his short life. With all due respect, he's never had a home, not a steady one. I intend to give him that."

The judge nodded thoughtfully. "You can provide for him there?"

"Yes. I have two sisters, and we run a guest ranch—"

"I've read the reports, Ms. Scanlon."

His impatience nearly crushed her, but she refused to bow. "Then you know that between the three of us, Jacob will be well cared for. We intend to give Jacob the family life he deserves."

Something that might have been respect came into the judge's gaze, and hoping herself ahead, Delia sat down, trembling.

The judge turned to Scott. "I'd like to speak to you, Mr. Felton. Privately. In my chambers."

Everyone remained silent as Scott rose. He and the judge disappeared for what was the longest three minutes of Delia's life. When they returned, both with inscrutable expressions, Delia thought her nerves were as shot as they could get. Then Jacob rose to his feet.

"I want to talk," he said in a voice that quavered.

"All right," the judge said very kindly, smiling at him. "I think that's a great idea. In my chambers. Follow me, son."

"But—"

"It's okay, Jacob. It's just that I think I should hear what you want to say privately first, that's all."

Jacob chewed his lip and followed the judge, for what turned out to be the second-longest three minutes of Delia's life.

When they came back, Delia searched both their expressions and was relieved to see Jacob looking relaxed.

Before she could try to figure out what that meant, the judge spoke to the courtroom. In his opinion, he said, there was no other choice.

Jacob belonged with his half sister, Delia Scanlon.

For a long moment, Delia just sat in her chair, surrounded by Edna, Jacob and Cade, stunned with disbelief.

Scott stood and quietly left the room, never even looking back at her or Jacob. She hardly noticed.

Jacob was grinning from ear to ear and trying to be cool at the same time. "I guess I'll have to do chores with the horses every day, huh?"

Delia stared at him. He was hers. Oh, God, he was really hers! She hugged him. "What did you say to him?"

"That it should be my choice, and I wanted to be with you."

Unable to speak, Delia just hugged him more tightly, then hugged Edna, who was smiling from shiny eyes.

"It was the right decision," Edna whispered in Delia's ear, holding her close. "And I'm so glad." She leaned back and smiled. "But save a spot for me. I'll want to come visit."

"I'll take good care of him," Delia promised.

"Oh, darling." Edna's smile was gentle. "It's not just Jacob I want to see. It's you, Delia. I want to see you, too." She cupped Delia's face in her thin elegant hands. "I'm so happy for you. I've carried around guilt for some time, for not being available when you needed me all those years ago."

"You didn't know," Delia said, touched beyond being able to hide her feelings. "I've never blamed you."

"Well, I've blamed myself. It'll never make up for those years when you were alone, but at least now, I feel some sense of justice has been served."

It felt odd to realize it, but justice *had* been served. There was some pride about that, not having been forced to come down to Scott's level and fight dirty for what she wanted. Who would have believed that she had so much love in her heart, when she'd always been satisfied with just having Maddie and Zoe? Now she had Ty, too. And Jacob. And they both belonged.

Cade reached for her hand then, giving her a

smile that had her quivering with things she didn't fully understand.

Did she have room in her heart for him, too?

"It's over," he whispered softly, pulling her aside so they could be alone.

"He didn't even question my ability to take care of him," she murmured. "Not a word about my worth, or—"

"It's no trick, Delia." He was watching her with that familiar intensity, and with something else, too. "Jacob is going home to the Triple M."

Home. Yes, the Triple M was definitely home. "And what about you?" she asked softly. "You've always been held to the Triple M by your promise to Constance Freeman, which you've fulfilled now. You're free to roam as you please, without ties."

His eyes were dark, eloquent. "Yes. I'm free of that promise."

"So?" she pressed, needing an answer. "Where is your home now?"

"Why did you let me make love to you last night?" he asked, instead, his voice low and direct. "Why me, when you'd never let anyone else?"

"I…"

"You let me think it meant the world to you."

"It did."

"No, not if you can look at me as you are right now, as if you expect me to walk out on you."

"It did mean the world," she whispered, closing her eyes. "It meant everything. I've never wanted

anyone the way I wanted you, and I needed…''
She shut her mouth and opened her eyes, stunned
by the sudden realization.

He came to the same conclusion at the same
exact moment. ''You needed me. It was a first for
you, this needing thing, and it makes you so unsettled and afraid that you can't accept it.''

''Cade—''

''No, you'll hear me out, dammit. You're one
of the strongest women I've ever met. No one in
their right mind would think of you as a user, as
weak or needy. But that's not good enough for you.
You have to shoulder your problems all by yourself.''

''I've always done that. It's just…easier.''

''Don't you get it? I don't want you to take on
the world by yourself. I want to be there for you.
I want there to be an *us*.''

''You do?''

''I've loved you from the moment I went into
the kitchen of the Triple M that night and found
you alone and crying, and trying to be strong
enough to carry the world's weight on your shoulders. I knew right then and there that the connection between us was something I needed, that it
was a soul and heart connection, one that couldn't
be denied.''

''Cade—''

''Oh, believe me—'' his smile was wry, and her
heart twisted ''—I tried to ignore it, but…''

''Cade…'' *He loved her.* The knowledge made

her stagger, so that she had to sink into a chair. Because she couldn't breathe, she put her head between her knees, her vision wavering. "You…you really…"

"Love you," he finished for her, his hands on his hips, a frown on his face. Relenting, he stroked a hand down her trembling back. "I can see that thrills the hell out of you. You need to breathe, Delia."

"I'm trying," she muttered, her heart and thoughts racing. He expected her to return his love, of that she was quite certain.

"Hey!" Oblivious, Jacob leaped into the chair next to her, still grinning. "We can leave now. We can leave right now and be at the ranch before dark, right? You going to give me a job so I look official when there's guests? 'Cause I figure I can lead out the horses for the rides, you know? You think I'm big enough for that?"

Delia peeked at him from between her fingers, her head still lowered, and had to smile, though she had to draw air into her lungs to do it. "You're looking a little excited there, champ. You sure you don't want to play hard-to-get a little bit longer?"

A flash of chagrin crossed his face, but it was fleeting. "Can I have the window seat on the plane?" He glanced at Cade. "Can I?"

Cade ruffled his hair fondly, but his smile was sad, his gaze on Delia. "I'm betting the window seat is yours," he said. "You take good care of those horses."

He isn't going with us, Delia thought. He was saying goodbye. She rubbed her chest above her aching heart, knowing it was all her fault, knowing all she had to do was reach for him and give him those three little words right back, and he'd come with them. For always.

Always. Always. Always.

The words echoed in her head like a mantra.

"Aren't you coming with us?" Jacob asked Cade, surprised and clearly disappointed. Now that he finally had family, he wanted them all with him all the time. He turned to Delia, confused. "Why isn't he coming?"

Because I don't know how to ask him to. She didn't know what to say.

Apparently Cade didn't, either. He said nothing, but she knew she'd never forget the look on his face, the pain in his expressive eyes, the tension that gripped his body as he hunkered down and gave Jacob a big hug. "I'll see you," he promised.

"Are you two fighting? Why? I don't want you to fight."

"We're not," Delia soothed. "We're just…"

"Breaking up?" Jacob asked, horrified. "Are you?"

Delia hadn't any idea that Jacob had understood the complexity of her and Cade's relationship. "Jacob, this isn't the time or the place to—"

Cade lifted Jacob's sagging chin. "I told you I'd see you. And I will. No matter what."

Without any of his usual hesitancy, Jacob con-

tinued to allow Cade's embrace. He even returned
it. "Pinky promise?"

Cade linked their fingers and they did some
elaborate arm movement, faces solemn. "Pinky
promise," Cade whispered back.

Then he was gone.

Gone. Right out of her life, just as she'd let him
believe she wanted.

Delia sighed and flopped over in her bed for the
hundredth time. It was two in the morning and
sleep wasn't anywhere to be had.

It wasn't Jacob. His warm reception from Maddie and Zoe had thrilled him. So had the job Ty
had given him, which was to feed the horses. He
was thriving.

It wasn't the ranch, either. They were going to
be full again this weekend, and with the latest
storm, which had dumped a couple of feet of fresh
snow on them, the guests would have their winter
wonderland.

Her sisters were both great. Maddie was clearly
in her element running the kitchen, and Zoe...well,
Zoe wore a permanent stupid-looking grin on her
face that widened at the mere mention of her new
husband.

Delia sighed and turned over yet again, because
she knew darn well what her problem was. It was
just over six feet tall, about 180 pounds of solid
utterly unforgettable male named Cade McKnight.

Neither of her sisters had been happy with her

to find Cade gone. Maddie had been kind enough to give her one long-suffering sigh, while all the while making it clear she thought Delia foolish for letting him go.

Zoe hadn't been nearly as kind. She'd come right out and told Delia she'd made a huge mistake to let her pride ruin everything.

But to imagine swallowing her pride and telling Cade she was wrong, that she did need him, she did want him, more than anything in the entire world…she didn't know where to begin.

And yet, lying there alone and chilled to the bone because she didn't have his warm loving arms around her was far worse, and she thought maybe if he walked into the room right now, she would be able to find the right words.

The same thoughts still haunted her the next morning at the crack of dawn. Staggering into the kitchen, desperate for caffeine, Delia whimpered pathetically at the smell of coffee already on the counter.

"God bless you, Maddie," she muttered, pouring herself a cup.

"Morning, Delia."

She nearly dropped her cup, then whirled around. Cade stood by the far wall, his own mug in hand, casual as you please. He was even smiling, though it didn't quite meet his eyes.

"What are you doing here?" she asked, when what she really wanted to do was throw herself at him, feel his arms come around her and haul her close. She wanted him to kiss away all her fears and doubts so that there was nothing left but the heart-and-soul connection she'd had only with him.

But she didn't make a move toward him, nor did he toward her. "I have a job here, at least for the moment, remember?"

Yes, she remembered. She didn't know why she'd expected him to walk away from it. She should have known that Cade, like her, had changed. Just as she'd learned to let people inside, he'd learned to not blame himself for his family's death. As a result, he would never walk away from something he started, especially not at the Triple M, not when he cared so much about her sisters and Ty.

"I'm taking two of the guests on a snowmobile trip today," he said. "We're cruising the back country, going to tear up some of this new snow."

He looked so good standing there, in his snow-mobile gear and boots, with attitude written all over him. *Tell him,* the voice inside her head urged. *Tell him all the things you promised yourself you would tell him if only you could have the chance.*

But before she could open her mouth, he crossed to the counter, set down his coffee and headed for the door, almost as if being with her was too much to bear.

"Cade?"

He didn't even look at her. "Have a good day, Delia." Then he was gone.

Four hours later, with no warning whatsoever, a rogue storm hit.

At the ranch house, the windows rattled and the lights flickered.

Radio contact with Cade was abruptly lost, which at first was no cause of concern. Everyone knew they were fully equipped to spend the night out in the wilderness, if they needed to.

The storm took a turn for the worse, and unforgiving and fierce, it raged on. Everyone in the house, including the two guests' wives, bit their nails as the wind and snow pelted the house.

They lost power, and the opaque darkness felt all-consuming, even more so because everyone knew there were three people out in that storm, people they cared deeply about.

Ty had the generator up and running in no time, but nerves were strung tight as everyone worried.

Actually ''worry'' didn't come close to describing what Delia felt—''terror'' was more like it— and she didn't draw a single breath without thinking about Cade, out in this dangerous storm.

To help occupy their thoughts, Delia dragged out her old beauty supplies and gave the wives manicures, but it didn't help ease her own fear one bit. Still, the women were suitably distracted with the service. So were two of the other guests.

Zoe and Maddie jumped on the opportunity, showing off some of Delia's designs and hand-made clothes. Every single female guest ordered something.

Ironic, Delia thought, with more than a little bitterness, that she'd found her niche on the ranch, that she finally had worth, that she actually felt as if she belonged—and none of it mattered. Not without Cade.

She made her way down the hallway to the kitchen, where she stared out the window into the wicked storm.

Please be okay, she prayed silently. *Please come back to me, safe and sound. I'll never push you away again. I'll even tell you how I feel, without hesitation.*

"Delia, honey, you okay?"

Delia didn't have to turn to see Maddie's face to know that she was deeply worried, too.

"I want him back, Maddie. I want him home and dry and warm and not hurt."

"You love him."

She felt Maddie's arm slip around her waist, and because she could, she leaned on her sister's shoulder. It felt good to be able to do that. "I let him leave angry and hurt," she whispered, her throat tight. "I can't believe I did that."

"You can tell him when he comes back. He is going to come back, Delia. You won't lose him, not now that you've learned to let him love you."

Delia's vision blurred as tears gathered. "I…I didn't tell him."

"He knows."

But Delia was sure he didn't; she'd been too stingy with her affections for him to know. And as the long day continued, she did her best to keep the guests and her brother busy. For Jacob, that wasn't too difficult, this ranch living was new enough that everything was an adventure. When she ran out of fingernails to paint, she switched to toenails. Her sisters enjoyed it, too; she could see the approval in their eyes. Even Jacob thought she was cool.

But she wanted Cade.

The truth was, she loved him with all her heart, and she was pretty sure she had since he'd first flashed his killer smile. No, she would never have control over him—or the elements, she thought with another wry glance out the window. She wouldn't be able to control her future, either, but she thought that was okay, maybe even good, because wasn't risk-taking a part of life?

Of course it was, and that it'd taken until now to see it made her angry at all the time she'd wasted. And as the day dragged on into night, and the night dragged on, too, tearing at her nerves, she used every excuse possible to stay glued to a window, torn between fear and anticipation, because she couldn't wait to have Cade back at the ranch and have the chance to tell him what she should have told him long ago.

Chapter 16

It was a morning of new beginnings, Cade told himself, as he and the two guests he'd taken out the day before rode their snowmobiles toward the ranch.

The day was glorious, the sun on the newly fallen snow making it shimmer like a sea of crystal.

It was almost as if the raging storm had never happened. But yesterday, Cade had found himself many miles from anywhere, completely responsible for Mike and Tim, two winter novices. They couldn't ride back, not in the whiteout, it was far too dangerous.

Thank God he hadn't caved in and taken Jacob as the boy had wanted. Cade broke out into a sweat just thinking about it.

In the end, they'd done all right, thanks to the emergency kit Cade always carried in his backpack and his ability to dig them a warm cave beneath a clump of trees.

But they were hungry, wet, cold and exhausted as they rode within sight of the Triple M. It was early—they'd headed out before dawn, as soon as the storm had broken—but every light in the ranch house was on and blazing a bright welcome.

When they were close enough to see clearly, Cade saw everyone standing in the yard, waiting anxiously. And when they came to a stop, Mike and Tim were mobbed by their wives, who'd no doubt been terrified by the experience.

Cade regretted that, just as he regretted his radio failure. But he couldn't regret the experience, he thought, as he looked at Delia, standing on the porch, apart from her sisters and Ty, watching him as though if she blinked he might disappear.

Maddie and Zoe flung themselves at him, hugging and crying and laughing and talking all at the same time. Even Ty gave him a hug, and Cade knew a barrier had been crossed in his own mind.

He let go of his past. He'd never forget, but he could let go, and most important, he had room in his heart to love again.

Unfortunately the woman he wanted didn't want that love, but he would survive that, too.

He broke away from the happy group to head inside, wanting food, a shower and sleep, and not necessarily in that order.

Delia was still standing there on the porch, and as he moved past, his body brushed hers.

"Cade?"

God, that voice. In all his life, no matter where he ended up, he knew he'd never forget her.

When he looked at her, she said, "I'm so glad to see you."

Great. He was dying here at the all-too-welcome sight of her. He wanted to shake her and demand she love him back. He wanted to grab her close and never let her go.

And she was "glad" to see him. "Me, too," he managed. "I'm going in."

He made it upstairs to the room he'd been given before letting his weary body sag with more than just the physical exertion. It was seeing her again, because the terrible yearning she always caused in him hadn't diminished. He flung off his clothes and let them stay where they fell, then stepped into the adjoining bathroom for a shower. He was so shaky that he wasn't certain he shouldn't sleep for a year first, but the promise of hot water warming his chilled body was too much to pass up.

He stayed under the hot spray until he felt too weak to remain standing. When he staggered out, he ran directly into Delia.

They both nearly fell to the bathroom floor, but he managed to catch her and keep them upright. "Delia—"

"Shh." She covered his lips with her fingers. With her other hand, she flipped off the light.

He was naked and dripping all over the floor, which left him feeling at a sore disadvantage, even without the light. ''What's going on?'' he asked, removing her fingers from his lips.

''I need to talk to you.'' Her voice faltered a bit when she stepped closer and brushed against his damp body.

''In the dark?''

''Just at first. Cade, I...''

She broke off unsteadily, and he knew she'd come close enough to realize he'd gotten aroused. Angry at his own inability to control his body, he tried to turn away, but she held him close, taking his hips in her hands and backing him with her until she was against the bathroom counter.

''What are you doing?'' he asked, all the more baffled when she slid her arms around his neck and brought her body flush to his. ''Delia—''

Her kiss cut him off, and what happened next was another sort of storm, equally powerful. He felt a blinding flash of need, an intense heat in his loins and a surge of love for her. With a groan of surrender, he gave in.

Before he could draw another breath, Delia had ripped her sweater over her head and undone her jeans. ''Here,'' she said. ''Right here. Please, Cade, love me.''

''I do. I do.''

''No, I mean...'' With a soft sound of need and impatience, she ran her hands down his chest, then lower, cupping him, dragging a moan from his lips.

He thrust into her hands, and she fumbled with her belt. Coming to his senses enough to help, he slid the jeans down her legs and lifted her off the floor.

"Hurry," she whispered.

"Hold on, then," he managed. "Hold on to me...there, oh, yeah, just like that."

Then, using the counter for leverage, he entered her, making them both cry out at the unbelievable connection. "I have to see you."

"Cade—"

"Have to," he said stubbornly, and reaching out, he flipped the light back on.

And if he thought himself aroused before, at just the feel of her, it was nothing compared to how he felt now that he could see her. Everything he felt was mirrored in her eyes—hunger, passion and a driving need he wanted to hear her admit, but knew she never would.

She closed her eyes, to hide from him, from this.

"No, no, sweetheart, don't. Open your eyes. Watch."

She blushed but opened her eyes and kept them open, seeing the love he couldn't hold back.

"Now tell me." With an effort that had him quivering, he stayed still. "Tell me you want me."

"I want you," she responded immediately, holding on to him for dear life.

"Tell me you need me."

She bit her lip, and when he withdrew almost

all the way from her body, controlling her pleasure, she protested with a small cry.

"Tell me, dammit. Tell me now when I'm buried inside you and there's nothing between us but this." Slowly, torturously, he slid back into her, then withdrew again, and when she whimpered, arching toward him, he thrust hard. "Tell me."

"I need you." Her fingernails dug deeper into his back. "I didn't understand this," she gasped. "Not until now. Don't stop loving me, Cade."

"I won't." His voice was like gravel, his body primed and ready, so that when she tossed her head back and started to shudder, he couldn't hold himself back.

Long after the pulsing ended, his body continued to tremble, but it had nothing to do with his adventure in the wilderness and everything to do with holding Delia in his arms again, feeling her against him and knowing he wasn't ever going to get over her.

Delia was sagged against him, still damp and panting. Uncertain he could even move, much less get them both into the bedroom, Cade brushed her cheek with his and murmured her name.

She relaxed her legs and slid down his body, then lifted her head to let him see into her teary eyes.

"Hey," he whispered, gently sliding his fingers over her face, his heart twisting. "Oh, baby, I'm sorry. Did I hurt you?"

"You're killing me." At his horror, she let out

a sound that was half laugh, half sob, and tightened her arms and legs around him. "I thought it mattered who I was, where I came from," she whispered. "It mattered to *me*, you know, and because of that, I was certain it mattered to you, too."

"Delia—"

"No, listen. Please, listen. I thought I was a nobody whose own parents didn't want her. Then when I found out I wasn't the heir, I felt even worse."

"I don't care where you come from. I never did."

"I know," she said in awe, cupping his face. "You just...love me. No matter what. I still can't quite believe it."

"Believe it," he said. "I always will."

"Oh, Cade..." There were tears in her eyes again and he nearly swore. But then he saw the smile curving her lips, the hope and love shining in her eyes.

"I *do* love you, Cade McKnight," she murmured. "In spite of myself, I do. And you know what?" Her voice broke and she drew a long unsteady breath. "I always have."

"I want forever," he said with steel conviction. "I want it with you."

"Forever sounds good to me." Her tears fell freely now. "Can we start right away?"

The fist around Cade's heart loosened for the first time in weeks, maybe years. He hauled Delia close and hugged her. "Right away," he said.

''Right now. Besides, I'm just where I want to be. *Home.*''

''Home,'' she echoed.

* * * * * *

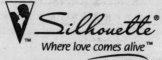

Look Who's Celebrating Our 20ᵗʰ Anniversary:

Celebrate 20 YEARS

"In 1980, Silhouette gave a home to my first book and became my family. Happy 20ᵗʰ Anniversary! And may we celebrate twenty more."

—*New York Times* bestselling author
Nora Roberts

"Twenty years of Silhouette! I can hardly believe it. Looking back on it, I find that my life and my books for Silhouette were inextricably intertwined.... Every Silhouette I wrote was a piece of my life. So, thank you, Silhouette, and may you have many more anniversaries."

—International bestselling author
Candace Camp

"Twenty years publishing fiction by women, for women, and about women is something to celebrate! I am honored to be a part of Silhouette's proud tradition— one that I have no doubt will continue being cherished by women the world over for a long, long time to come."

—International bestselling author
Maggie Shayne

INTIMATE MOMENTS®
Silhouette®

Visit Silhouette at www.eHarlequin.com.

PS20SIMAQ2

INTIMATE MOMENTS®
Silhouette®

presents a riveting 12-book continuity series:

A YEAR OF LOVING DANGEROUSLY

When dishonor threatens a top-secret agency, twelve
of the best agents in the world are determined to uncover a
deadly traitor in their midst. These brave men and women
are prepared to risk it all as they put their lives—
and their hearts—on the line.

Be there from the very beginning....

MISSION: IRRESISTIBLE by Sharon Sala
(July 2000)

She was there to catch a traitor, and getting passionately
involved with stubborn, sexy East Kirby was *not* an option for
Alicia Corbin. But then she discovered that the brooding
operative—whom she'd been instructed to bring back to the
field—was the soul mate she'd been searching for. Now if only
she could make her mission a success—and East a partner for life!

A YEAR OF LOVING DANGEROUSLY:
Where passion rules and nothing is what is seems....

*Available only from Silhouette Intimate Moments
at your favorite retail outlet.*

Silhouette®
Where love comes alive™